A GEORG

LITTLE STOLEN MEMORIES

CHERYL BRADSHAW

NEW YORK TIMES BESTSELLING AUTHOR

This book is a work of fiction. Names, characters, places, businesses, and incidents either are the products of the author's imagination or are used in a fictitious manner. Any similarity to events or locales or persons, living or dead, is entirely coincidental.

First US edition May 2024
Copyright © 2024 by Cheryl Bradshaw
Cover Design Copyright 2024 © Indie Designz
All rights reserved.

No part of this publication may be reproduced, stored, or transmitted, given away or re-sold in any form, or by any means whatsoever (electronic, mechanical, etc.) without the prior written permission and consent of the author. Thank you for being respectful of the hard work of the author.

*No man has a good enough memory
to be a successful liar.*
—*Abraham Lincoln*

1

Cora Callahan kicked back in the worn leather recliner, smiling as she watched her friends dance to Usher's "Yeah!" in the living room. The plan to take a trip with Brynn and Aubree before the trio headed off to separate colleges in the fall had taken weeks to put in motion. Once the arrangements were made, Cora moved on to step two: convincing her mother to allow her to take a weekend trip without parental supervision. It took some finagling, but in the end, she'd done it.

Her parents believed the three of them were spending the weekend at the beach.

In truth, they were nowhere near it.

They were in the woods at Cora's grandmother's summer cabin.

And they weren't alone ... their fellow classmates Aidan, Jackson, and Owen had joined them.

It was the perfect getaway for what Cora was sure would be a weekend none of them would forget. Brynn was dating Aidan, and Aubree was dating Jackson. That left Owen, who had been Cora's next-door neighbor since they were seven.

Cora and Owen had shared many memories over the years, and

in recent months, her feelings for him had begun to change. What started out as a childhood friendship had blossomed into something more, and Cora found herself struggling to decide the best way to tell him. She was ninety percent sure Owen shared her feelings. But that stubborn ten percent kept her lips sealed, and she'd pushed her feelings down, down, down until she'd all but convinced herself she no longer had them.

Tonight, it was all about to change.

Tonight, she'd tell him everything.

Thinking about it now, her heart raced.

"Come on, Cora," Aubree said, waving her over. "Dance with us."

Cora looked at Aubree, whose long, blond hair was bouncing up and down to the beat of the song, and said, "I'm waiting for Owen."

"You don't need Owen in order to dance," Aubree said.

"I know. It's just ... we're supposed to go for a walk."

Aubree glanced outside. "In the dark?"

"We have flashlights. We'll be fine."

"Where is Owen, anyway?" Aubree asked. "I haven't seen him for a while."

"He was outside earlier," Jackson said. "He went to get his glasses. He left them in the car."

"When?" Cora asked.

Jackson shrugged. "I dunno. Been a while, I guess."

Cora shot out of the recliner and walked to the door, opening it, and flicking the porch light on. She cupped a hand to the side of her mouth and shouted, "Owen? Are you out here?"

She was met with silence.

Poking her head outside, Cora glanced in all directions, shouting his name a few more times. When she got the same results as before, she pulled a mini flashlight out of her pocket and clicked it on, shining it in the direction of Owen's car.

Nothing suspicious there.

Still, she was beginning to worry.

She stepped back inside the cabin and said, "If he was out there, he isn't now."

"What did you say?" Aubree asked.

Cora walked over to the stereo and lowered the volume. "Owen's not outside. I mean, he's not answering when I call his name."

"Have you tried looking upstairs?" Jackson asked. "Maybe he's in his room. Brynn and Aidan are in theirs, spending ... ahh, time together."

"You can say they're having sex," Aubree said. "We're eighteen, for heaven's sake."

Cora walked upstairs and noticed Owen's door was closed. She knocked on it, waited a minute, and then opened the door, peering inside. Sitting on top of the bed was a coat and a thick pair of socks. Hiking boots were nearby on the floor, which made sense. He could have been preparing for the walk they'd planned.

A wave of concern turned Cora's insides.

If he wasn't here, and he wasn't outside, where was he?

The door across the hall opened, and Brynn stepped out. She smiled at Cora and said, "Hey, what's everyone doing?"

"I can't find Owen," Cora said. "When did you last see him?"

Brynn ran a hand through her short, auburn hair. "Ahh ... I haven't seen him since we arrived, I guess. It's not a big cabin. He's gotta be around here somewhere."

Cora hoped Brynn was right, and she did another sweep of the cabin, looking in closets this time.

Owen was nowhere to be found.

Cora asked everyone to gather in the living room to talk about what to do next, and Jackson suggested the girls remain inside while he and Aidan searched outside.

Twenty minutes turned into forty, and the teen boys still hadn't returned.

"Something's wrong," Cora said. "They should have been back by now. Maybe we should call our—"

"No," Aubree said. "If we call our parents, it's all over. They'll kill us for lying about where we are this weekend. I don't know about you two, but I'm not interested in being grounded all summer."

"I get it, but I'm scared," Brynn said. "I want to call my mom."

Cora considered their situation for a moment and said, "Give me a little time. If I don't find them, we'll make some calls."

"You're going outside?" Brynn said. "You're crazy. Who knows what's out there?"

"Well, I'm not just going to sit here and just hope they come back."

"Fine," Aubree said, "I'll go with you."

"No way," Brynn said. "You're not leaving me alone, and I'm not going out there."

"Aubree, you stay with Brynn," Cora said. "Give me fifteen minutes. If I'm not back, call your parents."

Cora grabbed Owen's coat off his bed and then walked to the kitchen, fishing a bigger flashlight out of the drawer. On the way out, she remembered her grandmother always kept a pair of night vision binoculars behind her jacket. She located them and stepped outside. The forest was quiet tonight, much more so than she remembered it being in years past. It was almost like it had been suppressed somehow, like all the life within it had stilled.

She descended the cabin's steps and started down the dirt road, shouting, "Jackson? Aidan? Can you hear me? Owen? Is anyone there?"

When no response came, she lifted the binoculars to her eyes and scanned her surroundings. She saw nothing unusual at first, and then she noticed a hand reaching up from the forest floor—a hand that appeared to be waving at her.

Cora rushed in its direction and found Jackson, his head bloody, eyes fluttering open and closed.

She knelt beside him, grabbing his hand as she said, "Jackson! What happened?"

"Hit me, and I ... I fell. Need ... go home. You ... out of here."

"I'm going to get help. I'll be right back. I promise."

Cora jumped to a standing position. She started for the cabin, and someone stepped out of the shadows, striking her on the side of the head with a heavy object. As her legs buckled beneath her and she sagged to the ground, she looked up, staring in confusion as her surroundings went black.

2

20 Years Later

It had been a quiet couple of weeks at the office. So quiet, I'd given my partners Simone Bonet and Lilia Hunter, some time off until business picked back up again. I'd enjoyed the quiet for a few days, but now I felt restless, waiting for a new investigation to get my blood pumping again.

I was sitting at my desk, staring at Luka, my Samoyed, whose head was nestled atop my feet as he snored away. The office door jingled, and Luka sprang up, staring at the woman who'd just stepped through the door. She was tall with long, blond locks and a curvy figure. She removed her mirrored sunglasses and glanced around the room, smiling when her eyes met mine.

"Is this the Case Closed Detective Agency?" she asked. "I didn't see a sign out front."

The sign was above the door and would be hard to miss, a fact I decided not to mention.

"It is," I said. "Can I help you?"

"I'm looking for Georgiana Germaine."

I walked over and introduced myself. "I'm Georgiana."

We shook hands, and she said, "My mother is friends with your Aunt Laura. Laura suggested I stop in to talk to you. I'm looking for information on someone from my past."

"I investigate homicides, but if you're looking to find someone, I can set up a meeting for you with Lilia Hunter, one of my partners. She specializes in that kind of thing."

She shook her head, saying, "Oh, no. I don't think you understand. The person I want you to find ... well, I don't know how else to explain. About twenty years ago, my best friends were murdered. The case was never solved, and I can no longer live with that."

The thought of a new murder to investigate shouldn't have excited me as much as it did, but I couldn't deny the feeling of elation I was experiencing.

"Why don't we have a seat?" I suggested. "And you can tell me all about it."

She walked over to my desk and sat down.

"What's your name?" I asked.

"Cora Callahan."

Cora Callahan.

I knew her story well.

Everyone in Cambria did.

The teenage murders were the biggest tragedy to ever happen in Cambria's quaint town. Six kids who'd just graduated from high school had arranged to meet up at a cabin for a fun weekend before they all went off to college. Within hours of their arrival, five were murdered, and one, who was left for dead, managed to survive—the very one sitting in front of me now.

"I know your story," I said. "What happened to you and your friends was before I became a detective for the San Luis Obispo Police Department. It was a cold case I'd always wanted to look into, but I'm sorry to say I never got the chance."

Cora stared down at her hands, clenching them like she was trying to get them to stop shaking. "For a long time, I didn't even like to think about what happened back then. Every time I did, I'd just get frustrated. There's so much I can't remember about that night."

There'd been many rumors around town after the murders. Some believed Cora knew a lot more than she was saying. Others thought the incident was so horrific, she'd found a way to block it out.

"Not long after the murders, you moved away," I said. "I'd heard you vowed never to return. Are you living in Cambria again?"

"Not living—visiting."

"For how long?"

She shrugged. "Hard to say. My father was just diagnosed with ... well, I'd rather not go into the details of it right now. I'll just say he's not going to be around much longer."

"I'm sorry."

"Yeah, me too. I've been back for a few weeks now, and even though I've done everything I can to make him my primary focus, I can't stop thinking about that night at the cabin."

I flipped my notepad open and grabbed a pen. "What can you tell me about it?"

"I have these flashbacks, moments where I remember something I didn't before, but it's all in pieces in my mind. I don't know how else to explain it." She leaned back in the chair. "The worst of it is, I can't separate fact from fiction. I'll recall something vague, and I can't be certain whether I invented it in my mind or it's something that happened."

"Trauma has a way of playing tricks on our minds. I bet a lot of what you remember has at least some basis in the truth."

"Before I get into it, I guess I should make sure you're willing to take the case."

I was willing all right, and I couldn't wait to dive in.

"Of course I'll take your case," I said.

Cora breathed out a sigh of relief and said, "Good. Your aunt says you're the best. She said you've solved every case you've ever had, even cases the police couldn't solve."

I remained still for a minute, trying to decide how to respond to her comment. At the time of the murders, my stepdad, Harvey, was one of the detectives who'd worked on the case. I remembered him discussing the case with me. Not being able to solve it before he retired had been one of his biggest regrets.

"Cold cases offer their own set of challenges," I said. "But I, for one, love a challenge."

"I'm glad to hear it. What information do you need from me?"

I thought about the best way to get her to talk about the events from that night. "You said you have fuzzy memories. Let's try and piece them all together like you're telling it to me in a story form."

She nodded, and it looked like she was about to speak. Then she clasped a hand to her throat and said, "Sorry. My throat ... it's a little dry."

I hopped up and walked over to the kitchenette, scouring the top shelf of the refrigerator for options. "We have water, soda, kombucha. What suits you?"

"Water is fine."

I grabbed her a bottle of water and a kombucha for myself, and I returned to my desk, handing her the water as I sat down. She twisted the cap off, drank half of it down, and then set the bottle on top of the desk.

"It was supposed to be the best weekend of our lives, you know?" she said. "I'd been psyching myself up to tell Owen about my feelings for him. We'd lived next door to each other since we were kids. I'd always considered him a friend until our senior year of high school."

"What changed?"

"I don't know. Comments from my friends, I guess. They teased me, saying they thought we had a thing for each other and wouldn't admit it to ourselves. And then one day, I realized they were right."

"Did you get the chance to tell him before ... what happened?"

"I didn't. After his funeral, his sister reached out to me. She told me Owen told her he wanted to ask me out on a date. It's too bad we never got a chance to see if we could have been more than friends. It took me a long time to admit to myself that I had feelings for him, and when I did, he was just ... taken from me in the worst possible way. It doesn't seem fair."

"It isn't," I said. "I know about your case. I seem to recall there were six of you at the cabin that night."

"Yeah, and I was the only survivor. It feels awful, you know, that they died, and here I am, still living."

"Your survival touched everyone in this town. When people found out you were alive, it was like a bright light shining through the darkness."

"I've always worried the man who attacked me would come back for me one day. I've spent the last two decades looking over my shoulder, and I'm tired of it. I'm so tired. It isn't any way to live."

"No, it isn't," I said. "I'll find the bastard, and together, we'll make sure he pays for what he did."

My quip about how I'd "find the bastard" went over well. Cora cracked a slight smile, and what's more, she looked at me like she was feeling something she hadn't felt in a long time—*hope*.

"I'll tell you everything I can remember about the night at the cabin," she said, "As long as you understand I can't always separate fact from fiction."

"No problem. Leave what's fact and what's fiction to me."

"All right. Where do you want me to start?"

"From the beginning, the moment the six of you arrived at the cabin."

Cora crossed one leg over the other, closing her eyes a moment, thinking. "We were so happy that day. Happy to be together. Happy we'd fooled our parents into thinking we were at the beach and not at my grandmother's cabin. It seemed like a perfect start to a perfect weekend."

Until it wasn't.

"Aubree and Jackson were dancing together in the living room," Cora said. "Brynn and Aidan were upstairs. I was sitting in my grandmother's recliner, and Aubree said something about not seeing Owen for a while."

"How long had it been since you'd seen him? Can you remember?"

"I'm not sure. Jackson said Owen had gone outside to get something out of the car, so I opened the front door and looked out, but I didn't see him anywhere. I started to panic, and I decided to search the house. When I still couldn't find him, the five of us met in the living room, and Jackson and Aidan decided to search outside."

"What happened next?" I asked.

"When Jackson and Aidan didn't return to the cabin, we discussed calling our parents."

"And did you?"

Cora shook her head. "We should have. It was a mistake. I wish we would have locked every door and every window and made those calls."

"Please understand I am not judging your decision when I ask you this, but what kept you from calling your parents?"

Cora pressed her head into her hands. "It was my fault. I made the decision. Aubree was worried if we told our parents where we were, we'd all be grounded for the summer, and we wouldn't be able to see each other. I suggested I'd go and look for the guys, and I said if I didn't return in fifteen minutes, then we'd call."

"Tell me what you remember happening after you left the cabin."

"It was dark, hard to see anything. I'd taken a flashlight and my grandmother's night vision binoculars, but even then, it was still difficult."

"What did you see and hear?"

"I remember how quiet it was—too quiet. I'd been going to my grandmother's cabin ever since I was a kid, and it had never been as quiet as it was that night. It was almost as if all the critters in the forest had all run away. I decided to look through the binoculars, and that's when I thought I saw something move."

"What did you think it was?"

"I had no idea, at first. Part of me was scared. The other part was filled with adrenaline. All I was focusing on was finding Owen and the others. So when I saw movement, I just ... I ran toward it."

"What did you find?"

"Jackson. He was on the ground. Blood was everywhere. It looked like he'd been hit on the side of his head, but there was so much blood, it was hard to tell what was going on."

"Was he alive?"

"Yeah, and he was trying to talk to me, to tell me something ... warn me, I think."

"Do you remember what he said?"

"I remember his mouth moving, and me crouching down. I said something to him, but I'm not sure what. I just remember how I felt, like I needed to get back to the cabin, to Brynn and Aubree, and we all needed to get the hell out of there. At some point, I remember standing. I looked toward the cabin and started running ... and then ... and then ... *he* was there. He was right there in front of me."

Cora pressed a hand to her chest as if struggling to breathe.

"Take a few sips of water," I said. "And please, take your time. If it's too much to talk about, we can stop for now and pick this up again later."

"No, I want to continue. I have to—for them. All these years of hiding, I should have been stronger. I should have pushed to keep the investigation open until the killer was found, and I ... I didn't."

"You want my opinion? You're being too hard on yourself. You went through a lot back then, and you've carried it with you all these years. It's understandable you'd want to step back from society after what happened. I get it. I've taken a step back myself before."

"Yeah, well ... even if you have, it looks like you managed to get your life back together. I haven't. I'm a recluse, only going out when I have no choice. I guess the way I look at it is part of me died along with my friends that night. I've never found a way to get myself back."

"You're here," I said. "I'd say it's a step in the right direction. There's no right or wrong timeline on finding yourself again."

She nodded and went quiet, and I waited, hoping she'd find a way to finish the conversation she'd started. There was so much more I hoped to ask, but I didn't want to push—not too hard, not if she wasn't ready.

Cora took a few more sips of water, seeming to come back to a state of normalcy, and then she looked me dead in the eye and said, "The man, he was just there, you know? He came out of nowhere. I remember he had something in his hand, but it was hard to tell in the dark ... a baseball bat or a big piece of wood, maybe."

"Did he say anything to you?"

"Not before he hit me. But after, when I was lying on the ground, he crouched down beside me, and I swear he whispered something in my ear. I figured he thought I was dying. Maybe I was ... I don't know how I survived when everyone else didn't. The doctor told my parents the impact of the hit I'd taken wasn't as hard as it was for the others."

I jotted a few notes down, read what I'd written, and said, "Going back to the man, is there anything else you can remember about him?"

"One minute he was there, the next I was hit on the head, and I went down." Cora swept a few locks of hair to the side of her forehead, revealing a scar. "Nothing like having a constant reminder of the worst night of my life."

"Do you have any recollection of what happened after he hit you, other than the man bending over you and speaking to you?"

"I think I passed out. I don't know how long I laid there, but at some point, I woke up. I didn't move for a long time. I worried the man was still there somewhere, watching me. After a while, I worked up the courage to stand, and I made my way back to the cabin as fast as I could. I thought about Aubree and Brynn and hoped they were alive, but when I opened the door and stepped inside, that's when I ... when I saw them, lying side by side on the floor in the living room. Dead."

4

"They were all dead," Cora said. "Everyone but me."

Nothing I could say would ease the pain she'd experienced then and was still experiencing now, so I said the only thing I could think to say: "I'm sorry."

Sorry didn't fix things.

Sorry couldn't change the past.

Sorry couldn't ease her pain.

But it let her know I cared about what she'd been through.

"I still have nightmares about what happened that night," Cora said. "I see Jackson, and Brynn, and Aubree. My nightmares are so vivid. They take me back to that night, and I find myself reliving what happened all over again."

I crossed my arms, thinking about what it must have been like for her that night. Terrified, lying on the ground, wondering if the killer was still lurking around somewhere, waiting for the opportunity to strike again.

"What did you do after you found Aubree and Brynn?" I asked.

"I ran to the kitchen and grabbed the sharpest knife I could find. Then I called my parents. As I explained what happened, my mom became frantic. I couldn't even understand what she was saying at first. She put my dad on the phone, and he told me my grandmother kept a pistol in the bottom drawer of her nightstand. He told me to get it and to lock myself in my grandmother's room, because it was the only room in the cabin with a deadbolt."

"Did you do it?"

She nodded. "I never even knew my grandmother owned a gun until my father told me. I'd never liked guns, but I knew how to shoot."

"How?"

"My family went camping a lot when I was in high school. My dad would save pop bottles for our trips, so we could use them for target practice. He knew I didn't like guns, but he encouraged me to learn how they worked anyway."

"How far was the cabin from your parents' house?"

"About an hour. Waiting for my parents to show up was the longest hour of my life. I remember sitting on my grandmother's bed with the gun pointed at the door, worried the killer would jiggle the door handle, break through the lock, and come for me a second time. But he never did. I figured he thought he'd killed us all."

A fortunate misjudgment on his part that saved Cora's life.

"If I remember right, your father called the police, and Harvey Kennison was the first to arrive at the cabin," I said. "He was one of the detectives who worked on your case. He's also my stepfather now, though I presume you know that."

"I do. Yeah, he got there a lot faster than I thought he would, about ten minutes before my parents. When he got the call about what was happening, he was closer to the cabin than they were."

"Did he wait for backup before he entered the cabin?"

"I don't think so. I remember hearing a door slam downstairs, and then a man started shouting my name. He said he was a detective with the San Luis Obispo Police Department. I remember hearing his footsteps as he walked up the stairs, and then he approached the door and knocked on it. He asked if I was inside the bedroom and if I was all right."

"What did you say?"

"I didn't respond at first. How was I supposed to know if he was who he said he was or if he was someone else? He let me know my parents were on their way along with some of his fellow officers. He said it was okay for me to open the door, but first I asked him to slide his badge under the door so I could prove he was telling the truth."

"Did you let Harvey in after he verified his identity?" I asked.

"I did. I threw my hands around him and started sobbing. It was the first time I allowed myself to believe I was going to make it out of there alive."

Cora closed her eyes, taking a deep breath in.

"Thank you for explaining all of this to me," I said. "I know it's not easy to talk about such a painful memory."

"It's not, but I know how important it is for you to have every detail I can remember."

Indeed.

"Who owns the cabin now?" I asked.

"It's still in the family ... except we haven't been back there since the murders happened."

"Any idea where I can get my hands on a key?"

"I'm sure my parents have one somewhere. I'll make a copy and get it to you right away."

"Harvey has mentioned your case to me a few times over the years. He's always regretted not solving the murders before he retired."

"My mother told me he still stops by their house every once in a while to ask how I'm doing. It means a lot to me."

"Yeah, he's one of the good ones."

I tapped my pen to the desk, thinking. "Who all knew about your plan to go to the cabin that summer weekend?"

"No one except the six of us, as far as I know. We made a group decision not to tell any of our other friends at school because we didn't want anyone to be upset that they weren't invited. Plus, we worried if we told anyone, our parents might find out we lied to them."

"Why did you lie to your parents?"

"Our parents didn't know the boys would be joining us for the weekend. They would have never agreed to it otherwise."

"Did any of you talk about the cabin trip in a public setting, somewhere people could overhear?"

"I didn't, but I don't know about the rest of our group."

Word about their plans had leaked somehow.

"You mentioned the person who attacked you was a man," I said. "I know it was dark, but is there anything you can remember about him? Approximate age, height, or any other relevant details?"

Cora considered the question for a moment. "I don't know. I never saw his face. He was wearing something over his head. Like a knitted hat, and the eye holes had been cut out."

"If you didn't see his face, how can you be sure it was a man who attacked all of you and not a woman?"

Cora tapped a finger to the top of the desk. "He was tall ... and big."

"When you say *big*—"

"I don't mean overweight. He was more muscular than flabby."

"Have you considered the man who attacked you may have been one of your classmates?"

"The police asked me the same question. I sorta felt like it was an older man? But I don't know for sure. I wish I did. I sat through so many interviews the first year after it happened, trying to remember anything I could to help them catch the guy. In the end, it didn't matter. Nothing I said made a difference."

Given her age at the time, it could have been easy for her to assume the man was much older. But she hadn't seen his face. And even though she had a faint memory of him speaking to her, she couldn't recall what he'd said. He could have been anyone.

"Could you make me a list of any classmates the six of you may have had a problem with back then?"

Cora leaned back in her chair. "It's been a long time. I'm not sure I can remember, but I'll try."

"Do you have a yearbook from your senior year of high school?"

"I think so. There are a few boxes of my things in my parents' garage. I'll go through them and see if I can find it."

"If you do, I'd like you to flip through it tonight, see if you can jog your memory. Make me a list of anyone you think I should talk to from your school days."

"All right. Anything else?"

I thought about what other things I might want to ask before I cut her loose.

"One more thing. I'd like to know where everyone was located when they were attacked," I said. "I know Aubree and Brynn were inside the cabin, and Jackson was outside, not far from where you were. Where were Owen and Aidan found?"

"The police found Owen around the side of the cabin. Aidan wasn't far from where I found Jackson. If I would have walked a bit farther, I would have seen him too."

"You were all attacked in the same manner ... blunt-force trauma, right?"

Cora sniffled and nodded, wiping a tear from her eye.

"The man who did this needs to be found this time," she said. "Being back in town takes me back to that night. In some ways, it feels like it all happened yesterday. I don't think I can handle dragging this all up again if there's not a different result."

I leaned forward and took her hand in mine, looking her straight in the eye as I said, "I'll make you a promise, right here and now. I'll give this case everything I've got. I won't stop looking until I find him."

5

"Well, well ... what a pleasant surprise," my mother said. "To what do we owe the pleasure of your company?"

She'd said it with a hint of sarcasm and a smile, and with the perfect dramatic flair I'd come to expect from her.

"Hi, Mom," I said as I opened the screen door. "I'm sorry I missed family dinner last night. Our flight was delayed."

A week earlier, I'd been in New York City with my fiancé, Giovanni. We visited his family and taken in the sights. Aside from it being the place where we both went to college and where he'd proposed, I'd always felt a bond to the city, its food, and its people. From the Staten Island Ferry to the bright lights in Times Square at night, there was a magical element to the place, a place which felt unlike any other.

My mother moved a hand to her hip, narrowing her eyes but not saying a word, and since uncomfortable silences had never suited me, I said, "Like I was saying before ... since I didn't make Sunday dinner, I wanted to stop by and say hello today."

Based on the look on her face, she hadn't believed a word I'd said.

"A visit from you is always welcome, dear," she said. "But I must say, I always know when you're not telling the truth. You've never had much of a poker face. Ahh, well. It's no matter. You're here now, and I've just put the kettle on. Care for a cup of tea?"

"I'd love one."

"Wonderful." She swished a hand in my direction. "Now get on in here before you let every fly in the neighborhood inside the house."

I closed the door behind me and followed her to the kitchen, where I found Harvey, sitting at the table filling in a word search.

He looked up at me and smiled. "Hello, Georgiana. Nice to see you. How's things at the detective agency?"

I glanced at my mother, who'd leaned in my direction, awaiting an answer.

"Oh, you know ... things at work are humming along," I said.

"Any new cases since I saw you last?" he asked.

I shifted my attention from Harvey to my mother, and I bit my lip, trying to decide how I was going to discuss the true reason for my visit. Ever since Harvey retired, my mother didn't like me discussing my murder investigations with him. She thought the stress of such topics spiked his blood pressure. When he was chief of police, it had, which was the reason he'd retired. Even so, he missed working on homicides, and he never hesitated to offer his help.

"I ... yeah," I said. "There's something I need to talk with Harvey about."

"Out with it, Georgiana," my mother said. "I'm guessing you have a new case. May as well get right to it and tell us what's on your mind."

I took a seat at the table, and Harvey pushed the word search to the side, giving me his full attention.

Knowing my new case would strike a chord with Harvey, I took a deep breath in and then said, "Cora Callahan came to see me today."

My mother, who was heading my way with cups of tea in each hand, gasped, and said, "Am I to assume you're talking about the woman who was almost murdered twenty some odd years ago?"

"I am."

"She's returned after all these years, eh?" she continued. "I cannot believe it. I never thought she'd show her face in this town again."

"Me either," Harvey added. "It's shocking, to be sure."

"Her father is ill," I said. "I don't think he'll be alive much longer."

"Oh, dear," my mother said. "I'm sorry to hear it. I'll stop in this week, see if there's anything I can do for Bette, her mother."

"You know Cora's mother?"

"We're in the same Pilates class, though she isn't as vigilant about attending as I am. I bet she's glad to have her daughter home."

Harvey ran a hand along his jaw. "That investigation haunts me to this day, as you well know, Georgiana. I've never been able to reconcile the fact that it wasn't solved, that I couldn't bring closure to all those families. They relied on me, and I've always felt like I let them down."

Knowing he felt the way he did ... well, it just made taking the case even more satisfying for me. If I could solve it, it would help ease his regrets about never being able to find the man the locals in town had named "the Cabin Killer."

"You did your best, Harvey," I said. "Maybe I'll get lucky and find something you couldn't before."

"I hope you're right," he said. "How can I help?"

"I'd like to talk to you about the interviews you had with Cora. What did she say back then when you questioned her?"

His expression soured, and he leaned back in his chair, lacing his hands behind his head. "The young lady was a mess back then. Never seen anyone cry as much as she did. Made it near impossible to get anywhere with my questions. Her recollection of the events was all over the place."

I thought my visit with Cora had gone well for a first interview. She'd been emotional here and there, but I could also see how time and maturity helped her process what she'd experienced in the past.

"I get the feeling Cora has blocked out certain aspects about the night of the murders," I said. "She admitted to having nightmares she can't seem to shake, but they're spotty and sometimes unclear, little stolen memories of a night she'd just as soon forget."

My mother, who'd been standing next to me, listening to the back-and-forth banter I'd been having with Harvey, set the cups of tea down and took a seat next to me. "Why did Cora come to see you this morning? What does she want from you?"

"Aunt Laura is friends with Bette."

"I had no idea."

"She stopped by the house the other day to see how Bette's been doing, and they got to talking about the investigation and what a shame it was that the case had never been solved. Cora learned I was a private investigator, and this morning, she came to see me. She's hired me to reopen the case."

My mother leaned back in her chair and crossed her arms. "After all these years, why do you think she wants to reopen old wounds? Seems a bit foolish to put herself through it a second time."

I didn't find it foolish at all.

I thought it was brave.

Cora was facing the demons of her past head on.

"Cora's never gotten the closure she needs and deserves, and I expect she never will until the man responsible for the murders is held accountable for his crimes," I said. "She's lived her entire adult life looking over her shoulder, wondering where he is now, and knowing he's out there, somewhere. In the back of her mind, she's always thought he'd come back for her one day to finish what he started."

"Must be awful, living in fear like that all this time," my mother said. "I cannot begin to imagine what she's been through."

Harvey ran a hand along his jaw and said, "There were so many oddities about the case. For starters, we never could establish a clear motive, or why someone would murder a group of teenagers and then just disappear without a trace. What was the reason? Why did he want all of them dead? I've asked myself these questions all these years, and I still haven't been able to make any sense of it."

"In my opinion, the motive behind the murders is personal in some way," I said. "It must be. I believe the killer knew the teens were going to be at the cabin that weekend, which leads me to believe the murders were premeditated. For whatever reason, he came for all of them. He wanted them all dead."

"I agree," Harvey said. "I thought the same thing when I was investigating the case."

"If we were dealing with a serial killer, even if he had a long cooling-off period, I would have expected him to resurface at some point and kill again. And he hasn't. Not in our county, at least."

It further strengthened my assumption that while killing three or more people could be considered serial killer behavior, the cabin murders had been different.

It led me to my next question.

"When you investigated the murders back then, was there anyone you interviewed or came across whom you suspected may have been the killer, but you just couldn't prove it?"

"We talked to everyone, and I do mean *everyone*. Everyone was a suspect—classmates, teachers, families—you name it. You know how it is when you start questioning people. The smallest flaw in anyone's story, and it's hard not to think they're guilty, even if there's not enough proof. What we lacked was evidence. We never had anything substantial enough to arrest any specific person."

In cases like this, it was hard not to get ahead of myself—to solve the murder based on a feeling that told me I'd found the killer, whether I had the proof to back it up or not.

"I understand," I said. "Still, I'd like to pick your brain, discuss your thoughts and feelings, anything you can remember."

"I have no problem going over it with you. You know how personal it is to me, even now. If there's anything I can do to help your investigation, I want you to know, I'm here for you, whatever you need."

Good.

Because there was something I needed.

"I'd like to get my hands on the case file," I said. "Since it's a cold case, I believe Foley won't have a problem letting me look at it. When I leave here, I'll stop by the department and see if I can talk to him."

Harvey offered a wry grin, scooted his chair back, and pushed himself to a standing position. "No need. When I retired, I made copies of all my files. Figured they might come in handy one day. Seems to me, today's the day."

"Now, just a second," my mother said. "I think Harvey and I should talk about this first."

"Darlene, you know how much I respect your opinion," Harvey said. "But this is something I need to do. It's important to me. I hope you can respect that."

My mother, who was almost never without a response, said nothing. She wasn't used to Harvey pushing back. She stared up at him, her expression changing from irritation to one of care and understanding.

Harvey left the room, returning a few minutes later with a hefty case file. He set it down on the table and said, "You let me know if you have questions about anything you see in here. I've been over this so many times, I've committed it to memory."

I took a few sips of tea, flipped the file folder open, and said, "It's been a long time since we discussed the case."

Harvey tapped a finger on the table and nodded. "It has been. As to your question before, there was one guy I leaned on a lot harder than the others."

"Who?"

"Danny Donovan. He was in his late twenties back then. He was renting a cabin not far from Cora's grandmother's place."

"What made you consider him a suspect?"

"He was an odd fellow. Reclusive. Fearful of law enforcement. We stopped by his place to question him, and as soon as he opened the door I noticed he had a bandage on his left index finger. I asked him about it, and he started shaking. Said he'd cut it working on a piece of furniture, of all things. Refused to say much beyond that. If he did do it, we couldn't prove it."

"Aside from Danny's demeanor and the cut on his finger, was there anything else about him that led you to believe he was guilty?"

Harvey bent down, flipped open the case file, and thumbed through it, pulling out a photo of a bloody, dented metal bat. He pointed at it and said, "We believe this was the murder weapon. And wouldn't you know ... we found it less than one hundred feet from the back of Danny's property."

6

I left my mother's house and called Simone and Hunter, asking them to meet me at the office to discuss the new case.

Hunter arrived on time, per usual, and Simone sauntered in about fifteen minutes late, per *her* usual. She plopped down in a chair and said, "From what you told me over the phone, it sounds like this case is going to be a juicy one. We haven't dealt with a cold case like this since we started the agency."

She was right.

We hadn't.

And I was up to the challenge.

"We're dealing with both the past and the present on this one," I said. "Solving a cold case won't be easy, but I'm confident we can do it."

"Well ... I, for one, can't wait," Simone said. "This is the first homicide case we've had in months. I've been dying for something like this to come our way."

Dying may not have been the most appropriate way to describe her excitement, but I could relate.

I spent the next several minutes sharing what I knew about the case so far. While Simone's enthusiasm grew the longer I spoke, Hunter remained tight-lipped, not saying a word, even after I'd finished talking.

I turned toward her and said, "How are you feeling about all of this, Hunter?"

She kicked her Birkenstocks to the side and leaned back on the sofa, thinking.

"I'm glad you took the case," she said. "I'm always up for helping people get the closure they need to move on. It's just ... I guess I can't stop thinking about what it must have felt like to be the sole survivor. I mean, can you imagine the guilt you'd feel to live after your friends have been murdered?"

"Cora's been through a lot," I said. "It makes taking this case even more meaningful and important. We have to solve it."

Hunter nodded. "Yeah, we do, and we will. I say we find this creep and nail him to the wall."

Simone and I exchanged surprised glances. Given the anxiety Hunter often had with cases like these, she worked behind the scenes, gathering information for us to follow up on. It wasn't often she made bold statements like the one she'd just made. I found it refreshing.

"I'm glad we're all in agreement," I said.

"Where do you want to start?" Hunter asked.

"I'd like us all to go over the case file Harvey gave me. Three pairs of eyes are always better than one. I might see or think of something you two don't, and vice versa. In the meantime, I've asked Cora to go through her old high school yearbook and to point out anyone who may have had a problem with her or her friends. There's also this Danny Donovan character Harvey told me about today."

"Who's he?" Simone asked.

"He lived near the cabin during the time the murders took place. When Harvey questioned him, he said Danny acted weird and shied away from saying too much. And get this—they found a metal bat, which they believed to be the murder weapon, not far from Danny's property."

"Sounds suspicious to me," Simone said.

"Yeah, but they couldn't prove he did it. I'll go through the case file tonight and make copies to pass off to the two of you."

"Is there anything I can do before then?" Hunter asked.

"You can find out where Danny Donovan is living now. I'd like to question him."

"What about me?" Simone asked. "What can I do?"

"I want you to look into the victims' families," I said. "I want to know everything about them—their backgrounds, what they were like as parents, what they were like as citizens of Cambria, what they're like now ... that kind of thing."

"I'm on it," Simone said.

"And I know it's been a long time," I said, "but I want to go out to the cabin and get a feel for the place, check out where each victim was found. You know, just poke around, see if anything speaks to me. Cora told me her family hasn't been out to the cabin since the night of the murders. She's going to get me a key."

"I bet it wasn't easy for Cora to come to you today," Hunter said. "Must have brought up all kinds of unwanted feelings."

"I'm sure it did, and that's why we're going to give this case everything we've got. Even though Harvey did all he could on the original investigation, I'm sure the victims' families feel somewhat let down by law enforcement. Let's make sure it doesn't happen again, *and* let's make sure Cora isn't looking over her shoulder for the rest of her life. These families need closure, and we're going to be the ones to give it to them."

7

San Luis Obispo Chief of Police Rex Foley leaned back in his office chair and laced his fingers behind his head, cocking his head to the side as he said, "So, let me get this straight. You were hired this morning to investigate a cold case, and you decided you'd drop by today to inform me just so I'm aware of it."

"Right," I said. "This case is twenty years old, which is long before the time you came to work for the department."

He narrowed his eyes. "What do you want, Georgiana?"

"What do you mean?"

"I don't believe for a second that you drove over here to tell me you're working a cold case. You could have spared yourself the visit and given me a call. And yet, here you are."

"I figured you'd hear about the case sooner rather than later, since my mother is aware of it. We both know it's impossible for her to keep anything to herself."

Foley snorted a laugh and said, "Would it surprise you if I said I already know about this new case of yours?"

It would not.

Foley was engaged to my sister, Phoebe, and given she and my mother spoke on the phone most days, I should have expected it wouldn't be long before news reached him. Still, it had been a mere two hours since I'd left my mother's house. She'd managed to spill the tea in record time. I didn't know what I felt more—irritated or impressed. I supposed it was a bit of both.

"All right, fine," I said. "I stopped by because I'd like to see what was taken into evidence during the investigation."

He laughed, shaking his head. "I thought as much. *If* you still worked as a detective for the department, I wouldn't have any problem with your request. You don't."

"Oh, come on. It's a cold case. What's the big deal? I have a copy of the case file."

Foley raised a brow. "How?"

"Harvey made a copy before he retired. And before you say anything, I'm coming clean about where I got it because you know what it feels like to have a case you can't solve. This one's haunted him for years. If I can solve it, it would be a win for everyone, the department and the families alike."

"If *we* could solve it, you mean."

I crossed my arms, glaring at him. "I don't follow."

Foley lifted a finger and then picked up the phone. He made a call and asked the person on the other end of the line to come to his office. Less than a minute later, Detective Amos Whitlock stepped into the room. He noticed me sitting across from Foley and a wide grin crossed his face.

Whitlock looked me up and down over his black, thick-rimmed glasses and said, "Well, hello, Georgiana. Wonderful to see you. Fine day we're having today, isn't it? Love the outfit. It's '40s era, if I'm not mistaken."

"You're right, it is '40s inspired."

Today I was dressed in a fitted, black, A-line skirt and a white blouse. Whitlock, who'd just turned seventy-one, was dressed just as sharp in a pair of black pants, a black turtleneck, a brown corduroy jacket, and shiny pointed black shoes.

Whitlock had come out of retirement about a year ago, when he learned the department was struggling to find a detective to replace Foley, who'd been promoted to chief of police. Whitlock had a long history of police work and had even worked alongside Harvey and my father. Since his return, we'd crossed paths on a couple of cases, and I'd come to enjoy the time we spent together.

Whitlock took a seat next to me and exchanged glances with Foley.

I wasn't sure why, but I was starting to feel uncomfortable.

"By the way you two are acting, I feel as though I've been left out of something," I said. "Would one of you care to fill me in?"

"I can explain," Foley began.

Whitlock raised a finger. "If you don't mind, allow me."

Foley muttered a few words under his breath, which I couldn't make out, but it was clear he did mind. Even so, he gave Whitlock the nod to go ahead.

Whitlock turned and faced me. "When I came out of retirement to work for the department again, I must admit my reasons were twofold. I knew you'd started your own detective agency, Georgiana, and I thought it might give us a chance to rub elbows every so often. You remind me a lot of your father, as you know, and I've missed him these many years since he passed away."

Whitlock was building up to something, his second reason for returning. And even though he hadn't admitted it yet, I'd figured it out—it was the reason the three of us were now gathered in his office.

"You worked with Harvey on the murder investigation all those years ago, didn't you—the one where Cora Callahan was the sole survivor?"

"That's right."

"And I'm guessing you've reopened the case."

"Right again. I never told you this, but it was one of the conditions I set before I became a detective again. We agreed when I wasn't busy working on another case, I could take another crack at this one to see if I could find anything new."

"Does Harvey know?"

Whitlock shook his head. "I'm not trying to keep it from him. I didn't want to say a word until I found a new lead. No sense getting his hopes up without a fresh angle, after all, something to crack the case wide open. And right now, I have nothing."

I sat in silence for a moment, taking it all in.

"Are you aware that Cora hired me this morning?" I asked.

"I'm just learning about it now."

"Does she know you're looking into the murders again?"

"Yes, she does."

I wondered why she hadn't mentioned it to me.

"What about the victims' families?" I asked. "Do they know?"

"Some do, some don't. I haven't been back on it for long."

I shook my head, looking at Foley as I said, "We have an interesting predicament, don't we? I've already accepted her case. What happens now?"

"Depends. How do you feel about it now that you know Whitlock is already working the case?"

I didn't know.

I hadn't had time to process it.

"I need to talk to Cora, to find out why she hired me when she knows the case has been reopened by the police department."

Whitlock placed a hand on my arm. "Way I see it, two heads are better than one, as they say. You and I ... we work well together, don't we? I have no problem with us both investigating the case on our respective ends and seeing what we can come up with this time around."

"I understand what you're saying, but I don't abide by the same set of rules that you do. It's one reason I quit this job and opened the detective agency. More loopholes. Less red tape."

"You do you," Whitlock said. "I'll do me. I don't see why it needs to change things. Do you?"

But it *did* change things.
It changed everything.

8

I stood on the Callahans' doorstep, trying to keep my temper in check as Cora gave me a nervous look, a look that told me she might already know the reason for my impromptu visit.

"We need to talk," I said.

"About what?"

"If I'm going to take your case, I need to be able to trust you."

"You *can* trust me."

"I need to know you're telling me everything, including the fact that Detective Whitlock reopened the case."

"I ... yeah. I should have told you."

"Why didn't you?"

Cora glanced over her shoulder and then stepped outside, pulling the door closed behind her.

"I ... I was going to tell you," she said, "and then I ... well, I guess I started worrying about what would happen if I did."

I moved a hand to my hip. "What did you think would happen?"

"I thought you might not take the case if you knew Detective Whitlock had decided to investigate the murders again. No offense, but he didn't catch the guy before, so I don't have a lot of faith in him solving it now."

Her reasoning was rational, but I still wasn't amused to find out I was the last person to know about it.

I blew out a long sigh and said, "From here on out, I need to know everything you know. Okay? If you can't do that, I can't continue working the case."

Cora tossed her hands in the air. "Look, I have enough to deal with right now with my dad, among other things. I'm not going to stand here being lectured by you. Work on the case or don't. I don't care."

But she did care.

I could tell just by looking at her.

She opened the front door and then slammed it shut, leaving me to wonder whether I was still working the case or not. I didn't feel like I'd come on too strong by approaching her about Whitlock, but maybe I had. I thought about knocking on the door and resolving the situation, but it had been a long day. I was ready to go home and sit in the hot tub, with a good book and a glass of wine.

With that in mind, I walked to my car.

Tomorrow was a new day.

I'd resolve my issues with Cora then.

As I reached my car, Aunt Laura pulled to a stop behind me. She took one look at me and leapt out of her Mercedes with a grocery bag in one hand and a can of Coke in the other.

Making her way over to me in a long, flowy, bohemian-style dress, she said, "Having a bad day, are we?"

"A frustrating day is more like it. I was just heading home. I'm thinking hot tub, wine, and a little mindless reading."

"Sounds like a wonderful plan," she said. "Before you go, want to tell me what has you so frustrated?"

I stood there, trying to decide where to begin. "Did you tell Cora to hire me?"

"Sure did."

"I'm assuming you know Whitlock has reopened the case," I said.

"Sure do."

"Are the two of you still dating?"

"Not *dating*. More like enjoying each other's company from time to time."

"Ohhkay."

She smacked me on the shoulder and said, "Don't look so surprised. I'm a modern woman. I don't care to live with anyone again, though I'm sure he'd be up for it if I were. I enjoy his company just as much as I enjoy my alone time. And there you have it."

Given her free-spirited nature, I should have expected as much.

"If you knew Whitlock reopened the case, why did you tell Cora to come see me?"

Aunt Laura's mouth opened, but as I waited for her to say something, she turned, her attention diverting from me to the silhouette of Cora peeking out the kitchen window at us.

"Look at her," Aunt Laura said. "She's like a frightened bunny in a hunter's trap. Scared of her own shadow. You met with her today. You must have seen it, heard the fear in her voice."

"I did. I know how hard it is for her to be in Cambria again."

"Harder than either one of us can imagine."

Aunt Laura was right.

No one would ever understand what Cora had gone through, what she was *still* going through.

"The question you should be asking yourself, kiddo, is what motivated her to meet with you this morning. Couldn't have been easy. And yet, she went outside of her comfort zone and pushed herself to do it."

I paused a moment, thinking back to my conversation with Cora. The more I thought about it, the more things were starting to make sense.

"Whitlock and Harvey conducted the initial investigation," I said. "And neither were able to solve it. I'm guessing Whitlock came over, excited to let her family know he was looking into the case again. But what faith would she have that things would be any different this time? In fact, she just told me those same words."

Aunt Laura moved a hand to her hip. "She'd have little faith, wouldn't you say?"

"If anything, I bet she's nervous about what will happen now that he's stirring it all back up again."

"I should say so. Think about it. She returned home to spend time with her father, and the first thing that happened when she arrived was her mother sitting her down to tell her Whitlock had reopened the case."

I thought about how I'd feel if I was in her position.

Cora deserved better, most of all from me.

"I imagine Cora's wondering if the killer is still lurking around here. She's probably asking herself how he will respond to the news that the case has been reopened. And what's more, what if he discovers she's returned to town after all these years to look after her ailing father? Will he come after her?"

Aunt Laura smiled, wagging a finger at me. "There she is—there's my brilliant sleuth of a niece."

"I was rude to her just now. I feel like a jerk."

"We all feel like jerks from time to time. It's human to err and so on. What matters is what you do about it now." Aunt Laura looped her arm around mine, and we started for the front door. "No use fretting over what's already passed. Come along, and all will be made right."

9

While Aunt Laura chatted with Cora's mother in the living room, I excused myself and found Cora standing in the kitchen, rinsing off a few dishes in the sink. She glanced over her shoulder at me, turned the faucet off, and dried her hands on a tea towel.

"I was hoping we could talk," I said.

She shrugged but said nothing.

"I'm sorry, Cora," I said. "I should have taken the time to look at things from your perspective, and I didn't. When I left the police station, I suppose I felt a bit humiliated because they knew something I didn't, and it bothered me. Still, I shouldn't have let it get to me the way I did. It was wrong."

"There's no need to apologize," Cora said. "I should have been honest with you. It's all right."

"No, it isn't. Working with you on this case isn't just about me being able to trust you, it's about you being able to trust me, and you *can* trust me. You can trust me with anything."

Cora leaned against the counter and said, "I know. Your aunt's told me a lot about you since I've been back in town. I knew coming to you was the right decision."

"Good. I'd like to begin again if that's okay."

"In that spirit, I have something for you. It took a fair amount of searching, but I found a key to the cabin. Follow me."

We walked down the hallway and into a bedroom. Looking around, it was like I'd just stepped into a time warp. The walls were painted two different shades of purple, a sharp contrast to the bright orange and hot-pink striped comforter on the bed. The darker of the two walls was plastered with photos torn out of magazines of popular actors and singers from the early 2000s—David Boreanaz, Luke Perry, and Francis Capra. On the opposite wall was a large *Gilmore Girls* poster.

Cora shot me a shy smile. "I know. It's like a time warp. Aside from boxing up a few of my things, my parents didn't change much in this room after I left town."

"Where did you go, if you don't mind me asking?"

"I have an uncle who lives in Spain. He has a casita he rents out sometimes, and he invited me to stay with his family for as long as I needed. I took him up on his offer and studied abroad for a while. One year turned into two, which turned into several years—the best years of my life. I suppose they were the best because over there, I felt far enough from this place to feel safe."

"What made you decide to return?"

"I missed my parents. They couldn't afford to visit more than once a year, and as time passed, it became harder and harder to be so far away."

She sat on the bed, and I took a seat beside her. "How long have you been back?"

"Guess it was 2009 or so. I moved to Lone Pine. In my first week there, I met a woman named Lelah. A couple of months later, we moved in together, and we've been roommates for the last ten years."

I'd heard of it before, but I'd never been.

"Lone Pine's in California, right?" I asked.

Cora nodded. "It's a five-hour drive from here, which makes it easy for my parents to visit. Well, it *was* easy before my dad became ill."

She went silent, and I waited, remembering how she'd hesitated when mentioning her father's illness at my office.

I didn't want to push.

"My dad's in the hospital," she said. "He ... ahh, he has late-stage pancreatic cancer. I guess he's known for several months, but my parents didn't know how to tell me. Doctor thinks he has three, maybe four months to live, at most. Anyway, let's talk about something else, okay?"

"Okay, sure."

I thought about the best way to segue away from the topic of her father, and I uttered the first thing that came to mind.

"How did you meet your roommate, Lelah?" I asked.

"At a self-defense class. She was the instructor. She's one of the toughest women I've ever met. I've learned so much from her." Cora pushed up from the bed and walked over to her nightstand, where she removed a key, which was dangling from a rainbow-colored wrist coil. "This was my key to the cabin. It was the ... uhh ... key I had the night I ... you know, the key I had with me that night. It's been buried in this drawer of junk ever since."

She handed it to me, and I slid the key into my handbag.

"Do your parents know I'm planning to go to the cabin to have a look around?" I asked.

"Yes, and they're fine with it. They have too much on their minds to be bothered with anything other than what my father's going through right now. I was passing by their bedroom the other day, and I overheard my father telling my mother his one wish before he passes away is for this case to be solved. It's one of the main reasons I decided to hire you."

"I will do everything I can to make that happen."

"I have to say, when I left your office this morning, I felt different, like a weight had been lifted. For the first time, I found myself thinking about what it would be like to move past the guilt I've carried from that horrible night. I can imagine myself living a normal life."

The guilt I've carried—a phrase I found interesting.

Cora had expressed guilt earlier over being the lone survivor of the attacks that night. But was there something more, an additional feeling of guilt she had not revealed to me yet?

"Before I take off, I thought I'd ask if there's anything else you've thought of that I might need to know," I said. "If there is, now is the time."

Cora walked over to a small bookcase near the closet and removed her high school yearbook from the bottom shelf.

"Have you had a chance to look at it yet?" I asked.

"I've started. What I've seen so far has brought back a lot of memories I've forgotten about. I know you asked me to look at my classmates to see who you should talk to, but I'm not sure I can get through it."

"Is there anything in particular that you found triggering or want to talk about?"

Cora sat down on the bed, flipping through several pages of the yearbook. She stopped, pointing at a photo of a teen boy. In the photo, he was in a classroom, stirring a pot of soup.

"This is Xander Thornton," Cora said. "We were in culinary class together."

I leaned in to get a closer look. What struck me first was the sheer size of the kid. Xander wasn't just big—he was professional-football player big, which set my mind ablaze. He would have had no problem wielding a bat—or any other object for that matter.

"Xander's a big guy," I said.

"No one in our school came anywhere close to his size."

"He doesn't even look like a high-schooler. If I saw this photo and had no other context, I'd guess he was in his mid-twenties."

"He was older than we were, I think. There were rumors back then that he'd been held back more than once. I don't know if the rumors were true, though. We were in the same grade, but we didn't grow up together. He moved to Cambria when he was in high school."

"Is there something you want to tell me about him?"

Cora nodded. "He was picked on a lot in school, which, given his size, is a surprise, I know. If he had defended himself, no one would have stood a chance against him."

"Who picked on him?"

"A few of the guys on the football team. Some of their girlfriends went along with it too."

I shook my head and said, "Why did they pick on him?"

"He wasn't like us ... he was different."

"Different in what way?"

"He just seemed a bit ... I don't know. Slow, I guess. Knowing what I know now, he may have been on the spectrum or maybe even had a mental health issue."

"What did the footballers do to him?" I asked.

She swallowed hard, turning away from me as she whispered, "They called him names and told him he was stupid. They'd do things like flick him in the back of the head when they passed him in the hall."

It disgusted me to hear about how he'd been treated.

Bullying was never okay, no matter what rationalization a person used.

"Did any of your friends who were at the cabin that night take part in the bullying?" I asked.

Cora went quiet for a moment, which gave me my answer.

Her eyes welled up with tears as she said, "I want you to know, *I* never said anything mean to him, not one disparaging thing. Aidan and Jackson were the ringleaders. They teased him the most, and I suppose Brynn and Aubree went right along with it. My friends ... they weren't bad people, you know? I mean, the way Xander was treated was wrong, of course. We were stupid teenagers, doing stupid things."

Her passive response wasn't enough.

It didn't excuse how they'd treated him.

Harm was inflicted, harm that may have impacted Xander's life in such a way that he'd plotted revenge—revenge on all of them.

"What about Owen, your next-door neighbor?" I asked. "Did he pick on Xander too?"

"Oh, no. Owen was the nicest, gentlest person I've ever known. One time, Aidan and Owen were walking together down the hall between classes. They passed by Xander, who was carrying a pile of books and papers. Aidan reached out and smacked it right out of Xander's hands. Everything went flying. Aidan laughed and kept on walking, but Owen stopped and helped Xander pick it all up."

While Owen may have been more sympathetic than his fellow classmates when it came to Xander, the fact remained he was still friends with those who'd bullied the poor kid, as was Cora.

Helping Xander pick up books was one thing.

Standing up for him was another.

And by the sounds of it, no one stepped in to stop what was going on.

"I need to ask you a serious question, Cora."

"You want to know whether I think Xander could be responsible for the murders."

"You must suspect him, or you wouldn't be pointing him out to me or telling the story you just did."

Cora's expression soured. "I didn't think he did it back then, but now ... I'm not sure."

"Why? What's changed?"

"I still haven't told you everything. The bullying ... it was just part of it."

The bullying was *part* of it.

I braced for what was to come.

"What do you mean?" I asked.

"Xander used to call us on the phone."

"I'm sorry, I'm not following."

Cora snapped the yearbook closed and said, "He used to call a few of us girls. When we'd answer, he'd breathe this awful, heavy breathing like he was out of breath, and then he'd whisper our names over and over again."

"Did anyone tell the police about the phone calls?"

"I don't know. I didn't."

"Did the caller say anything else, other than your name?"

"No."

"When did the calls begin?" I asked.

"Around the middle of our senior year."

"If he didn't say anything, how did you know Xander was responsible for making the calls?"

"For months, we didn't know who was doing it. We assumed it was Xander, but we didn't know for sure. We figured it out after a call he made to Aubree."

"What happened?"

"She confronted him."

"In what way?" I asked.

"During the call, Aubree challenged him to reveal himself, to tell her who he was and why he was calling. She said if he didn't, she'd never take another one of his calls again, and she'd make sure none of the other girls would either."

"How did Xander respond?"

"He didn't say a word at first, and then he asked her if she wanted to play a word game. She said yes. He told her he would give her a clue."

"What was the clue?"

"He said he was near the exit. Or at least, that's what she thought he'd said. After they hung up, she called me. She told me about it, and I stewed on it for a while. Then I realized if you take the letters in Xander's name and scramble them you get the word 'near.'"

"What about the exit?"

"I don't think he was saying 'the exit.' I think he was saying DX. Scramble NEAR and D and X, and you get Xander. Once we put it all together, we were sure he was the one making the calls. Aubree told Jackson. He told Aidan and ..."

Cora hung her head, going quiet.

"And what?" I asked. "What did they do?"

She slapped a hand against her mouth, speaking through her fingers. "It wasn't good. I didn't know. I didn't know it was going to go that far."

The guilt I've carried.

I was about to learn the true meaning behind those words.

"Whatever happened back then, no matter how awful it was, I need to know," I said. "It's important."

One minute went by.

I placed a hand on her shoulder, giving it a light squeeze.

Cora looked up at me and said, "All right. Aidan and Jackson invited Xander to hang out with them one night at the park. They told him they were sorry about how they'd treated him in the past, and they wanted to make up for it."

"I'm assuming Xander went?"

"He did, and we knew he would. If anything, I always got the impression Xander wanted to be accepted by the rest of us."

"What happened at the park?"

"They were nice to him at first. They'd taken a bottle of vodka from Aidan's dad's liquor cabinet, and the guys were laughing and doing shots together. Except, Aidan and Jackson were pouring themselves a single and not taking the whole shot. They were giving Xander *doubles*. After giving Xander a few shots, he was drunk, and

I mean, blackout drunk. I don't think he'd ever had liquor before. He passed out."

"What happened next?"

"Aidan and Jackson thought it would be funny to strip Xander's clothes off, down to his underwear, and they did. They leaned him against a tree and tied a rope around his waist. Then they dangled a piece of paper from his neck, a note that said he was a stalker and a pervert. The next morning, a jogger found Xander. He called the police. And that's not even the saddest part. Even after all they did to him, Xander refused to tell anyone who'd done it."

Thinking of what Xander had been put through, it wasn't hard to imagine the elation he must have felt to get an invitation to hang out with a couple of the most popular boys in school. Only to arrive and have his hopes dashed when he was stripped down to his tighty-whities and left for all to see. It was the ultimate humiliation.

"Aside from Aidan and Jackson, who else was at the park that night?" I asked.

"Brynn and Aubree ... and *me*."

And there it was—Cora's role in all of it.

Cora may have not assisted in what had happened that night, but she was there. She was there, and she did nothing.

"I would do anything to take it back now, to stand up for him," she said. "I'm so ashamed."

"We've all done things we're ashamed about. What matters is that we learn from our wrongdoings and strive to do better."

I handed her a few tissues, and she blotted her eyes.

Cora scooted back on the bed so she could lean against the headboard, saying, "I wanted to go back to the park after we left to untie him."

"Why didn't you?"

"I worried about how angry he'd be and what might happen if we were alone together."

"I know it wasn't easy for you to tell me what you just did. Thank you for telling me the truth. I have another question. Did you tell the police your friends were responsible for what happened to Xander at the park, after the murders happened, I mean?"

She shook her head. "I know it was a mistake. I was ashamed about my role in it all. Ashamed or not, I was scared, but it shouldn't have stopped me from telling the truth. It's the reason I'm telling you now. I meant it when I said I thought Xander was innocent back then."

"Seems to me he had a clear motive. Why didn't you consider him a suspect?"

"I was in the hospital during the funerals. I heard he showed up at every single one, and he cried at all of them. He cried like he'd lost his closest friends."

10

I sat in the hot tub with a glass of bubbly in hand, reflecting on the day. It wasn't long before Giovanni joined me. He scooted next to me, putting his arm around me. "What's on your mind? I can see the wheels spinning."

I took a deep breath in, nestled into him, and said, "It was a long day. I took on a new homicide case today. It's a cold case, one Harvey worked on back when he was a detective. I feel a lot of pressure to solve it, not just for the families who've been waiting for closure all these years, but for Harvey. I know how much solving this case would mean to him."

"Tell me about it."

I filled Giovanni in on what I knew so far.

When I finished, he said, "You're right. It is different than the other cases you've had since you started the detective agency. Given Harvey's personal connection, what are your thoughts on involving him in some way?"

I'd had the same idea ever since I left my mother's house. I couldn't stop thinking about the look in Harvey's eye as he discussed the case with me. It was like I'd just thrown him a bone. I had no doubt he was eager to be my sidekick if I wanted one.

There was just *one* sizable hurdle in the way.

"I want to involve him," I said. "Given the fact my mother pushed Harvey to retire as chief of police after his heart attack, I'm not sure what she'd say about me asking him to help with the case. I feel like she might pitch a fit over it."

"She might, but isn't it his decision to make?"

We exchanged glances and burst out laughing.

"This is my mother you're talking about," I said. "Since when does Harvey have a say about anything? He can't tie his shoes without her permission."

"Harvey has his moments. Your mother does too. I've seen it. She may give him a hard time, but I expect part of it has to do with the loss of your father. It may have been a long time ago, but it was the biggest loss of her life. She's protective of Harvey, and all of you. It's because she cares."

"She cares all right, enough to put a tracker on my car last year."

He gave me a squeeze and said, "Think about it from her perspective. You put yourself at risk every single day when you take on a murder case."

He was right.

Whenever I had cases like this, my mother checked in on me a lot more than usual. And that was saying something.

"I know my line of work isn't easy for her," I said.

"It isn't, and I don't expect it ever will be. On several occasions, your mother has expressed her feelings to me on the matter on several occasions. And yet, even though she worries, she's proud of you and the peace and resolution you bring to families each time you solve a case. She has a soft spot for your line of work, and I expect she knows how important the cold case is to Harvey."

Giovanni sat up, reaching for the bottle of prosecco I had chilling.

As he refilled my glass, I said, "You're right. It's worth a conversation. Harvey knows this case inside and out, as does Whitlock, I expect. If anyone can help me track the murderer down, it's those two. It's not about me, after all. It's about solving the case."

I heard a dinging sound, an indication that a vehicle was at the front gate. I glanced at the clock hanging on the wall. It was half past eight in the evening. Not too late for visitors, but I wasn't expecting anyone.

"Are you expecting someone?" I asked.

"I am not. Are you?"

"No."

"Better check and see who's here, then."

He hopped out of the hot tub, wrapped a towel around his waist, and reached for his phone to view the feed from our security camera. Then he looked back at me with a big grin on his face.

"Who is it?" I asked.

"There are a couple of gentlemen parked out front whose ears must be ringing."

A minute later, Giovanni showed Harvey and Whitlock inside. I toweled off and changed into vintage loungewear made of rayon—and a coral color I loved. Entering the living room, I greeted both men, and then took a seat on the couch.

"I assume the two of you are here to talk to me about the Callahan girl's case," I said.

"Right you are," Whitlock said. "Before we go down that road, can I pivot and address our meeting in Foley's office today? As soon as I learned Cora hired you to investigate the murders, I'd wanted to speak to you. It just so happens you stopped into the police station before I had a chance."

"I was surprised to learn you'd reopened the case," I said. "As you well know, but it's fine."

Whitlock crossed one leg over the other. "Is it fine? When you left, I got the feeling you were upset, which is the last thing I wanted to happen. We've had a good working relationship ever since I started back at the department, wouldn't you say? This case is important to me, but so are you."

"It's true I was irritated when I left the police department. I drove to Cora's parents' house, and we talked. Since then, I've had time to view everything from a different perspective. I know how invested the two of you were in this case and how hard it must have been when you weren't able to solve it. Bottom line, I'm not opposed to working together with you on it."

Harvey clapped his hands together, beaming with happiness as he said, "I'm glad to hear it. When you stopped by today and said you were taking Cora's case, I didn't think the day could get any better. But then Whitlock popped in and let me know he'd reopened the case as well. With the two of you on it, I can't sit around doing nothing. I want to be part of it."

"I appreciate your enthusiasm," I said. "I'm just wondering if you've spoken to Mom about it."

"I ... ehh, I have not. Leave it to me. I'm sure once I explain my feelings to Darlene, she'll understand."

Whitlock looked over at me, and it appeared he was thinking what I was thinking. While I'd always admired Harvey's positive outlook on life, speaking to my mother was not going to be as easy as he hoped.

"You need to tell her as soon as you can," I said. "By tomorrow morning, I'd say."

Harvey nodded, saying, "I agree, I agree."

"If we work together on this case, what does that look like to you both?" I asked. "What do you have in mind?"

Whitlock shot me a wink and said, "We're here to ask what *you* have in mind. Don't want to step on any toes, or fingers, or feelings, if you know what I mean."

I leaned back, thinking about the best way to move forward without getting in each other's way. "I'm the most comfortable when I work on my own."

"We're well aware," Whitlock said. "And we respect your methods, of course."

"What matters most is communicating with each other. The last several cases I've investigated have been alongside the police department, so I say we keep doing what we've been doing. We'll share what we discover with you, and you do the same."

"Works for me," Whitlock said.

"Me too," Harvey said. "What's your plan for tomorrow?"

"I'd like to interview a couple of the men who were related to the case back then. And I see no reason for us to speak to the same people unless we believe one of them is a viable suspect."

"Divide and conquer," Whitlock said. "I like it. We'll cover more ground that way. Who are the lucky fellows?"

"The first is Danny Donovan. Since the murder weapon was found close to the property line of the cabin he was renting, I'd like to question him. I want to see if his story is the same or if it has changed over time."

"And the second fellow?" Whitlock asked.

"Xander Thornton."

Harvey rubbed a hand along his jaw, thinking. "Xander Thornton. So familiar. Why does his name ring a bell?"

Whitlock snapped his fingers and said, "I remember! He's the tree kid."

"The *tree* kid?" Harvey asked.

"Yeah," Whitlock said. "Remember the high school kid who was tied to the tree at the park? Had a note wrapped around his neck, something about him being a stalker, if I remember right."

Harvey's eyes lit up. "Oh, yeah. I remember now. He refused to give the police any names. We couldn't understand it. Why are you interested in him, Georgiana?"

"I had an enlightening conversation with Cora this evening," I said. "She made a confession, something she's been keeping to herself for a long time."

Harvey learned forward and said, "Go on."

"Aidan and Jackson used to bully Xander at school. They are the ones who got Xander drunk and tied him to the tree."

"No, way," Harvey said, slapping his thigh. "Why are we just hearing of this now? Why would she keep such an important detail to herself?"

"Cora was at the park the night it happened. So were Brynn and Aubree. They may not have taken part, but they didn't stop Aidan and Jackson from doing what they did either."

"It never made any sense to us. Why tie him to the tree in the first place?"

"Cora, Brynn, and Aubree were all receiving prank calls at the time. Someone they assumed was a fellow classmate would breathe heavily into the phone while saying their names. During one of those calls, Aubree pushed the caller to reveal himself."

"Did he?" Harvey asked.

"In a way. The caller offered a scrambled version of his name."

Harvey and Whitlock stared at me in confusion. I explained what the prank caller had said and why Cora believed the caller had identified himself as Xander.

"Ever since Cora told me the story, it's been on my mind a lot," I said. "Just because the girls assumed Xander was the one making those calls, doesn't mean they were right."

"How so?"

"As far as I know, Xander never admitted to it. Anyone could have passed themselves off as Xander. Someone could have been trying to set him up or place the blame on him to shift it away from themselves. I assume most of their classmates knew Xander was being bullied, which makes him an easy target."

Harvey rubbed his chin, appearing to give my comments some consideration.

"I like your way of thinking," Whitlock said. "Out of the box, just like your father used to do. Never taking things at face value as they seem, but always digging deeper and wider to root out the facts."

There was no higher compliment than being compared to my father, who I believed had been one of the best detectives of his time.

"As soon as I have addresses for Danny and Xander, I'll be speaking to them, and I'll let you know when I do," I said. "In the meantime, I need to look over the rest of the case file, which I've decided to save until tomorrow morning. I don't have the mental capacity to focus on it tonight. What's your plan?"

"I suppose Harvey needs to speak to the missus," Whitlock said. "Then I'd like to speak to Silas about testing some of the items we still have in evidence. We're hoping he can find something we weren't able to before."

Silas Crowe was the county's medical examiner and a close friend. If anyone could find a way to breathe new life into the case with a piece of old evidence it was him.

"Good idea," I said. "Forensics has come a long way in twenty years."

"Well, it's getting late," Harvey said. "I best get on home before I get a phone call inquiring as to my whereabouts."

In truth, I was surprised my mother hadn't already called.

They stood, and Harvey turned toward me, a look of concern on his face. "Sometimes I feel you're better at talking to your mother than I am."

I felt for him, but it was something he needed to do on his own.

"You'll do just fine," I said. "Good luck. I'll speak to you both in the morning."

11

I was sitting behind my desk in my office, talking to Simone and Hunter about the previous day's events. I shared the big reveal—what Cora had said about her classmates bullying Xander. We discussed that somber news for a while, and then I explained the agreement I'd made with Whitlock and Harvey about teaming up on the case.

When I finished, Simone jumped right in, saying, "I didn't see that coming."

"Me either," Hunter said.

"We've worked with Whitlock on cases before," I said. "Seems like we never work homicide cases these days without the police department being involved somehow. Which makes sense, as much as I hate it."

"And here I thought because it's a cold case, we'd be working this one alone," Simone said. "I see your point though. They were the original detectives on the case."

"Including them isn't a bad idea," Hunter added. "I bet Harvey's excited to be back in the game after his retirement a couple of years ago."

All morning I'd wondered if he'd spoken to my mother yet. If so, I wondered how she'd reacted about his interest in putting his detective hat back on for one last investigation.

"Let's talk about today's agenda," I said. "Hunter, have you had any luck locating Danny Donovan?"

She reached into her bag, pulled out a piece of paper, and handed it to me. "It wasn't easy, but I found him. He's still in the area, living in a mobile home park in San Simeon."

San Simeon was fifteen minutes from Cambria, which was good news.

I slid Danny's address into my handbag and said, "I'll see if I can speak to him after we finish up here. Then I'll head out to Cora's grandmother's cabin. I was told they haven't been there since the murders."

"I'll see what I can find on Xander while you're gone," Hunter said.

"And I'll be speaking with the victims' families," Simone said.

The agency's front door opened, and in walked a woman I wasn't sure I was ready to see this early in the morning.

"Yoo-hoo, Georgiana, are you here?"

"I'm in my office, Mom."

Simone leaned toward me and whispered, "Ehh, I'm thinking we should go, leave you to talk to your mother alone."

I shot Simone a wink and said, "Abandon me if you must."

Hunter and Simone wasted no time exiting my office, and my mother sauntered in. She closed the door behind her, set a plate of quiche covered in plastic wrap on my desk, and plopped down on a chair in front of me.

"I see you're out and about early today," I said. "Thanks for the quiche."

"You have a big case ahead of you. I figured you'd enjoy a few slices of one of your favorite breakfast dishes."

We stared at each other for a moment, and I contemplated what to say next.

I assumed Harvey had spoken to her, and that was the real reason she'd stopped by my office unannounced.

"How's your morning been going?" I asked.

My mother raised a brow. "As if you don't know."

"I'm guessing you and Harvey have talked."

She brushed a few crumbs off her shirtsleeve. "Yes, dear. I know all about his desire to be involved in the case."

"And?"

My mother clasped her hands together, setting them on her lap as she said, "I believe we've come to an arrangement."

I was almost afraid to ask.

"What kind of arrangement?"

"One where I tag along."

Tag along?

She can't mean ...

"You're not saying you're going to tag along with *me*, are you?" I asked.

As soon as I'd blurted out the words, I realized my approach could have been much more genteel.

Too late now.

My mother swished a hand through the air. "Heaven's no, child. I mean, don't get me wrong, I would tag along with you in a heartbeat. Think of the fun we'd have. Mother and daughter, sleuthing together, catching the bad guy. I know you though, and I know you'd never allow it."

The disappointment on her face was loud and clear, but she was right. Having her along wouldn't be a good idea.

"When you say you're going to *tag along*, what do you mean?"

"Harvey made a strong case in favor of him assisting with this case, and I understand what it means to him. After all, it was his case. Including him is the right thing to do."

"I agree."

"Would you also agree that stressful situations take a toll on him?"

"I would."

"I can't bear to see him have another heart attack. His first one was ... well, scary. I have no interest in a repeat, and I said as much to Whitlock this morning."

"What did Whitlock have to say?"

"He asked if we could come to a compromise. We both gave it some thought, and Whitlock asked how I would feel about tagging along here and there whenever they were doing anything Whitlock thought might be harder on Harvey than he'd care to admit."

The thought of three senior citizens parading around town, trying to solve a twenty-year-old murder spree was part comical and part concerning. I had enough on my mind without worrying over what would happen if they found themselves in a dangerous predicament. But as I thought about how annoyed I felt when my mom fussed about my safety during my casework, I knew I was doing the exact same thing to her right now. It wasn't fair. If I could do it, so could she. The three of them together were the toughest senior citizen trio I knew. But I'd keep that to myself for now.

"I'm waiting," my mother said.

"For what?"

"For you to say something. I'm sure you have an opinion about my proposal. I can see it on your face. You don't like the idea, do you?"

"I need to give it some thought before sharing my opinion."

"We'll be fine. I'm still going to the shooting range from time to time. And I'm happy to report I'm the best in my class, or so I've been told."

I clasped my hands together, resting them on top of my desk. "Does Foley know about all of this?"

"He will. He's my next stop."

"What if he doesn't like the idea?"

"Doesn't like it? He's engaged to your sister, due to marry her next month. Do you think he has the nerve to say no to me, given I'm his future mother-in-law? I should say not."

"It sounds like you have everything all figured out."

"Yes, yes. It's well in hand." She pushed herself out of the chair. "Anyhoo, I just wanted to stop in and say how excited I am to be working together."

"But we're not ..."

I considered finishing the sentence and stopped myself.

"We're not *what*, dear?" my mother asked, eyebrow raised so high it just about disappeared into her hairline.

"Thanks again for the quiche. Let me know how it goes with Foley."

My mother stood, shaking her head as she walked out the door, saying, "No need. I'm sure it will all go as expected. I'll leave you now. Back to work ... toodaloo!"

12

The mobile home park where Danny lived in was full of campers, trailers, and tiny homes, all varying in size. While clean, the address numbers, which had once been stenciled on the curb in black paint in front of each residence, were faded to the point of being unreadable. Locating which lot was Danny's was not easy.

As I puttered my way around the park, I saw an older woman eyeing me. Her long, gray hair was swept back into a ponytail, and she was doing circles around the park on an aqua-colored adult-size trike with a white metal basket on the back. On her third lap, she pulled to a stop beside my car, using her knuckles to tap on the window.

I put my window down, and she said, "Are you looking for someone?"

"Danny Donovan," I said. "He's in Lot 48. Do you know him?"

"Sure do. What do you want with Danny?"

I thought about how best to answer the question and decided to keep it simple. "It's personal."

"Personal in what way?"

Keeping it simple didn't seem to be working.

"I'd appreciate it if you could point out his place of residence," I said.

She tapped a finger on the bike's handlebar and looked me up and down. "You're about the furthest thing from Danny's type, driving around here in your vintage Jaguar and fancy attire. I'm guessing you're not here for a good time. If you want me to tell you where he lives, I'm going to need more to go on."

My patience was wearing thin.

"I'm Georgiana Germaine," I said. "I'm a private detective. I just need to ask Danny a few questions."

"A private eye, eh? What's he done?"

"Nothing. Are you going to tell me which place is his or not?"

She moved a hand to her hip. "No, I don't believe I will."

"Fine. There are plenty of other residents who live around here. I'll ask someone else."

I started to put the window up, but she stuck her bony arm in to stop me.

"Now, wait just a second," she said.

"Why should I?"

"My name is Dorothy. Danny is my brother."

"Your *brother*? Why didn't you say as much in the first place?"

"Danny doesn't get a lot of visitors, not ones who look like you, at any rate. I suppose I can be overprotective at times, but why shouldn't I be? You've gone out of your way to tell me nothing about why you want to question him."

I was stunned.

I sat there as I tried to contemplate the best way forward.

Did I tell the truth?

Did I tell a partial truth?

Would it even matter whether I told the truth or not?

"As his older sister, I have a right to know why you want to speak to him," she pressed. "He doesn't like visitors much, and he doesn't like talking to people he doesn't know. I guess what I'm saying is, if you don't have a good reason for being here, you can just turn your car around and head right on out of here."

"How long have you lived in the area?" I asked.

"What's that got to do with anything?"

"If you answer my question, I'll tell you."

"All my life. I was born in Cambria. We moved around a bit. Lived in this mobile home park for the last ten years. Why?"

"Do you remember the teenagers who were murdered twenty years ago?"

"Who doesn't? Made national news. All sorts of people were hanging around town during that time. The Feds even got involved. Not that them being here made one bit of difference. The case was never solved."

"It wasn't, but I'm hoping it will be now. The case has been reopened."

Dorothy gasped, pressing a hand to her chest. "Why?"

"The victims' parents deserve to know why their children were murdered. I'm hoping to solve the case and bring closure to everyone involved."

"I think it's a marvelous idea. Whose idea was it to reinvestigate?"

In the interest of protecting Cora and the fact she was back in town, I said, "One of the original detectives who worked on the case came out of retirement about a year ago. He asked the chief if he could look into it again, and since there are no other homicide investigations going on right now, his request was granted."

"I see. How do you fit into the mix?"

"My agency has agreed to consult on the case."

It wasn't the full truth, but it seemed convincing enough.

"And this pertains to my brother how?" she asked.

"Your brother was living in a cabin close to the crime scene."

"I remember. Detectives spoke with him a few times. Don't think he was much help."

"I'm hoping if I talk to him he might recall something now that he didn't back then, something to help us solve the case this time."

Dorothy went quiet for a moment and then said, "I don't think he'll agree to talk to you, but I suppose it's worth a try. I've thought about those poor kids a lot over the years, and I've wondered how their families are doing. I imagine it's hard to go on living when you've lost a child."

It was.

A fact I knew all too well.

"Do you live with your brother?" I asked.

"Oh, no. We could never share the same space. We tried it once before. It didn't work. I'm a minimalist, and he's ... well, a hoarder. A clean hoarder, but a hoarder all the same. He lives a few doors down from me, which is the perfect arrangement. We both enjoy our personal space, but we do get together for dinner and that sort of thing."

She gestured for me to follow her. "Let's go. I'll take you to his place."

I drove around the corner, parking in front of a newer fifth-wheel attached to a large pickup truck. Danny may have been a hoarder, but the exterior of his place was well kept. There was a flower garden out front, and I didn't spot a single weed in sight.

Dorothy hopped off her bike, and we walked together to the front door. She knocked, and we waited. Danny opened the door, beer in hand. He took one glance at me, and his eyes widened. He looked to be in his mid-sixties, and he had salt-and-pepper hair, which was slicked back. He was an attractive man, though a bit on the rugged side.

Addressing his sister, he said, "Who's this, Dorothy... a friend of yours?"

"Nope, we just met. She's here to see you."

He took a step back, set his beer on a nearby table, crossed his arms, and said, "Why?"

"You remember those poor dears who died some twenty years ago?" Dorothy asked. "The ones who were murdered at the cabin?"

"What about them?" he grunted.

"The case was never solved."

"I'm aware."

"It's a shame, don't you think?"

"Get to the point, sis."

She lifted her chin in my direction. "This here is Georgiana Germaine. She's a private eye, and she's just informed me that the cabin murder case has been reopened. Can you believe it ... after all these years? Maybe there's a chance it'll be solved this time. Imagine what peace it would bring to the families."

Danny bent over at the waist, placing both hands on his legs as he struggled to catch his breath.

"Danny, are you all right?" Dorothy asked.

"I ... yeah, I'm fine. What does any of this have to do with me?"

Since it appeared he had no interest in addressing me, I cut in. "I have been asked to assist with the case. I understand you used to live in a cabin close to where the teenagers were murdered."

"What of it?"

"Do you remember the conversations you had with the detectives back then?"

"Nope. And even if I did, why would I want to talk about it again? It didn't have anything to do with me."

"You might not feel like you have any information to share," I said, "but sometimes the smallest thing leads us in a direction that changes everything. I'm not asking for much of your time. Just a few minutes."

"Yeah, well ... I'm busy."

"No, you're not," Dorothy said. "You're retired, and by the looks of it, all you have going today are a bunch of reruns and a six-pack of beer."

"You don't get it. The way they treated me, like I had information I wasn't sharing. Nothing I said satisfied them back then, and it won't satisfy them now. So, like I said ... I'm busy."

Danny attempted to close the door, and I pressed a hand against it.

"A metal bat was found not far from the cabin you were renting at the time," I said. "Right at the edge of the property. Do you have any idea how it got there? Did you see anyone suspicious in the area at the time or hear anything unusual on the day of the murders?"

Danny reached for a set of keys, which were hanging on a hook on the wall.

At first, I thought he was holding them out to me, until I noticed something dangling from the keyring. As I stood there, contemplating what he was about to do next, my eyes began to burn, the bubbling sensation blinding me.

I stumbled back, reaching for my gun.

But it was too late.

The damage had already been done.

13

Dorothy cursed at her brother, and then she brought me inside the fifth-wheel. She helped me to the sofa, and I sat down. I heard her shuffle away from me, and when she returned, she said she had a wet washcloth. She placed it over my eyes, telling me to hold it there while I waited for my vision to return.

A second before Danny pepper-sprayed me in the face, I'd jerked my head back. It didn't save me, but it kept me from getting a full dose of the spray. Still, my eyesight was minimal, at best. It would be some time before I could see well enough to get myself out of there.

While I sat there, helpless, contemplating my situation, Danny and Dorothy were in the kitchen, arguing over what had just happened.

"What in the hell is wrong with you, Danny?" Dorothy asked.

"*Me*? You're the one who brought a cop to my doorstep."

"She's not a cop. She's a private eye. Who she is or what she is doesn't matter. What matters is you maced her in the face, you moron. Do you know how much trouble you're in?"

"You don't understand," Danny said. "I can't go through this again. I won't."

"You can't go through *what* again?"

"When the murders happened ... well, let's just say there are things I never told you."

"I'm listening."

"The cops didn't question me once. They questioned me several times."

"Why?"

"I expect it's because they needed someone to pin the murders on, and I looked just as good as anyone. Once they found the bat at the back of the property, they started pressing me harder, asking the same questions over and over again."

"I'm sure they were just trying to be thorough."

"No, they were looking for someone to blame back then—and they still are," Danny said. "It sure as hell isn't going to be me."

"You've got it all wrong," Dorothy said. "Georgiana didn't come here to accuse you of anything. She came here because she has questions she was hoping to get answered."

"I'm not buying it. I bet she would have told you anything to get to me."

"I believe her, and what you did ... it wasn't right."

"You have no idea what I was put through back then. You've never been in a position where cops will say anything to trip you up, hoping you make a mistake and hang yourself. I was interrogated like I was a criminal, plain and simple."

"You're being paranoid, Danny. You've always been paranoid. If you didn't do anything wrong, you have nothing to fear."

"If I'm paranoid, you're naïve. You believe anything anyone tells you."

"Either way, you assaulted a woman, which makes you look guilty, like you *are* hiding something even if you're not. You've taken what could have been a simple conversation between two people and blown it way out of proportion."

It went quiet, and then I heard what sounded like someone pacing back and forth.

"Do you think I don't know what I've done," Danny said. "I didn't mean to ... I just ... when she started grilling me with her questions, I panicked."

"You did a lot more than panic."

"If the police are looking into the murders again, they'll question me too. And if they decide to place the blame on me this time, it won't matter if I'm innocent. I don't have the kind of money to hire a good enough lawyer to defend me, and that's how most innocent people get imprisoned."

Dorothy let out a loose, long sigh. "I know you don't have faith in the justice system. Maybe it's all the conspiracy theories you've let yourself believe over the years."

"They're not theories. My eyes are open. It's everyone else in society who chooses to go through life with theirs shut. Sheep! An entire society of sheep."

"I don't suppose anything I say will make much of a difference."

"It won't."

"Well then, what now?"

"I'm getting out of here," Danny said.

"Seems like an extreme thing to do under the circumstances. Where will you go?"

"I don't know. I can tell you one thing—I'm getting as far from here as possible."

The sound of heavy footsteps passed by me, heading toward the back of the trailer.

"I apologize for my brother," Dorothy said in my ear. "Don't worry. I'll be with you until all of this is cleared up. You're going to be fine. I'll make sure of it."

I had so many things I wanted to say, but until my eyes cleared up, now wasn't the time, so I said, "Thank you, Dorothy."

She shuffled away from me, moving in the same direction Danny had gone a minute earlier. I heard what sounded like a sliding door being closed and then whispers between the siblings. I leaned to the side, trying to make out what they were saying, but I couldn't.

I removed the cloth from my eyes and noticed I was starting to see things—fragments of objects around the room. It gave me enough confidence to reach back and pick my cell phone out of my pocket. I cupped it in front of me, leaning over as I pressed what I hoped was the number 1.

Holding the phone to my ear, I waited for the call to be answered.

When it was, I uttered a single word, "Help."

14

I'd always been a tough, independent woman. A woman who didn't always work well with others, even though I cherished the relationships I had with Simone and Hunter. We worked well as a team, in part because they knew how I operated, and they respected it.

And though I preferred being on my own during murder investigations, I no longer went out without a backup plan. Today's backup plan came in the form of the Find My app on my phone, which shared my exact location with Giovanni.

I suppose I could have called Simone or even Whitlock to come to my aid, but there were times when a heavier hand was warranted—a hand that didn't always answer to the law in the same ways others did.

Ever since Giovanni and I met in college, I learned he didn't come from an average Italian family. His family was ... in a word, *connected*. Nowadays, Giovanni's sister ran the family business, bringing it into the present in a more legitimate, though still profitable way. But family was family and protecting one another mattered above all else.

The fact Danny was packing a bag concerned me. I had questions. And I was determined to have them answered. If it meant leaning on Danny a bit harder after what he'd done to me, I was prepared to do it.

In my opinion, he deserved it.

What had been fervent whispers between brother and sister in the back room had morphed into an audible discussion I could hear.

"Please, Danny, don't go," Dorothy pleaded. "Talk to Georgiana. If you apologize, I'm sure she'd be willing to put all of this behind us and start again."

"She's not going to forgive me for what I did," Danny said. "She'll have me arrested. The cops will say I assaulted her, and I'll be locked up. End of story."

"Allow me to talk to her, at least. You were scared. You did what you did without thinking. It's not like you shot the woman. You pepper-sprayed her. There's no permanent damage, now is there?"

"She'll regain her sight any time now. I need to go."

As their banter continued, the camper's front door opened, and someone stepped inside.

I felt a hand on my leg, followed by Giovanni's voice in my ear.

"I am here, cara mia. What's happened?"

"I was pepper-sprayed," I whispered.

"By whom?"

For a moment, all was quiet, and I wondered if Danny and Dorothy had clued in to the fact we were no longer alone. I tipped my head to the right, indicating the direction Giovanni needed to go. He kissed my forehead and backed away, his voice commanding as he said, "My name is Giovanni Luciana. I'm armed, and I expect you to do as I say if you don't wish to be fired upon. You have five seconds to show yourself. Fail to do so, and I will use whatever force necessary to drag you out."

"Please, don't shoot," Dorothy said. "It's not what you think. I'm coming out. I'll explain everything if you give me a chance."

With each passing moment, my vision continued to improve. I turned to see Dorothy sliding the door at the back of the camper open, her hands raised as she walked toward Giovanni.

"It's not her you want," I said. "It's her brother, Danny. She's innocent. She was trying to help me."

Addressing Dorothy, he said, "What's your name?"

"Dorothy."

"All right, Dorothy. I'd like you to take a seat next to Georgiana."

"Of course. Can I just say something? My brother's not a bad person. Please, don't hurt him. He made a mistake. As you can see, we've been looking after Georgiana, staying with her until she could see again."

Her voice trembled, and I felt a smidgen of sympathy for the woman.

Giovanni said nothing, his focus on the sliding door to the back room. I heard what sounded like something, or someone, hitting the ground outside.

Danny must have tried to escape out a window.

Stupid.

As Giovanni rushed toward the back of the camper, I heard a scuffle happening outside. The camper's front door opened again, and Danny was shoved inside.

Behind him, Giovanni's main security detail offered Giovanni a smile as he said, "Thought you might want this one returned to you."

"Thank you, Santino," Giovanni said. "I can take it from here."

Santino nodded and closed the door.

Giovanni turned toward Danny, using his gun to gesture at the kitchen table as he said, "Now then, take a seat, and we'll all have a civilized conversation."

Danny was reluctant at first, but he did as Giovanni requested.

"Who are you?" Danny asked. "You don't look like a cop."

"I'm not a cop. I'm far worse, trust me. Now, before we decide what to do with the two of you, I wish to know what happened here."

Dorothy opened her mouth and Giovanni shook his head. "I don't want to hear from you. I want to hear from Georgiana."

"Sorry," Dorothy said. "I get ahead of myself sometimes."

I spent the next few minutes detailing what had happened since I arrived. I ended with the main event and the fact that Danny was planning to leave town.

Giovanni took a moment to take it all in and then said, "What would you like to do now?"

"I have some questions for Danny. I'm not leaving until they're answered."

I turned, addressing Danny. "I'll make you a deal. You answer my questions, honestly, and I won't press charges. Don't answer them, and I will."

"I ... I don't know," Danny said.

"You used pepper spray in a non-self-defense situation, which is considered a misdemeanor or a felony charge in this state. You could be facing a fine and a possible prison sentence of anywhere between sixteen months and three years."

Danny considered his options and said, "How do I know you're not lying?"

"Hearing your conversation with Dorothy minutes ago, I get the impression you have problems trusting the police. You seem to think everyone is out to get you. They're not."

"How would you know?"

"The men who questioned you after the murders took place—I know them ... well. And I can tell you without a doubt that if they had believed you'd committed the murders back then, they would have kept on questioning you until you confessed. The case meant a lot to them. All they're trying to do now is solve it. Same with me."

Danny leaned back in the chair, shaking his head as he said, "There was no reason for them to keep coming at me like they did. My story was the same the first time I told it as it was all the other times."

I could feel heat flooding my cheeks. I was about to lose my temper, and it was all I could do to rein it in.

"Is that so?" I shot back. Your story may have been the same, but why do I get the feeling you left something out? Oh, I know why. There's no point in running unless you did."

"I don't know what you're talking about."

"If you want to keep lying to Georgiana," Giovanni said, "I can get the police on the phone right now. I'll have them here in no time."

"What makes you think I'm not telling the truth?" Danny asked.

"The look in your eyes when you learned who I am and why I'm here," I said. "There was real fear in your eyes, the kind of fear I see when a person has something to hide."

"I didn't murder anyone."

"I might be inclined to believe you," I said. "*If* you tell me the truth."

Danny swished a hand through the air. "You'd say anything, I bet, if it means getting what you want."

"I don't say anything I don't mean. It's not who I am. I don't expect you to believe me, but it's true."

"It is true," Giovanni said. "You can trust her, and you should."

"Yeah, well, I don't believe either one of you."

I wasn't getting anywhere.

I went quiet for a moment, thinking of another way I could get through to him. Maybe I needed to go back to the beginning, to his original statement, see how he'd react when I questioned him about what he'd said to the police.

"I had a chance to look over your original statement this morning," I said. "I wanted to review it so I knew what questions to ask you today."

"Yeah, so? What about it?"

"On the day of the murders, you said you were at your place, working on a wooden chair to sell at your booth at the farmers' market the following weekend."

"As far as I recall, yes."

"In the notes it says Harvey, who would have introduced himself to you as Detective Harvey Kennison, went to the farmer's market the next weekend to see if you were there. You weren't. In fact, you'd shut down your booth and didn't return to it for over a year. Why?"

"If you think about it, it's obvious. I was shaken by what happened."

"Shaken by the deaths of teenagers you'd never met before? Shutting down your booth for as long as you did seems like a strong reaction, if you ask me. As you'd said, the crime had nothing to do with you."

"I didn't need to meet them to be affected by it. The fact it happened so close to my place was hard for me to take."

"So hard you moved out of the cabin you were renting and in with your sister for a while."

"My brother moved in with me because he was struggling to pay the rent," Dorothy added. "And as for the booth, he wasn't selling enough furniture to keep it going, so he took a break. Got a job that paid the bills."

Danny frowned at Dorothy. "I don't need you stepping in, Sis. I can answer questions myself."

"I'm just trying to help."

"You're not helping," Danny said.

Dorothy dropped her chin into her hand and looked away, muttering something about never being appreciated.

"You should treat your sister with more respect," Giovanni said. "The way I see it, she's trying to help."

He was right.

Still ...

"Let's try and stay on track," I said. "Had you ever seen or met any of the teenagers before they were murdered?"

Danny tapped a finger to the chair, averting eye contact as he said, "I ... no."

"I need you to look at me," I said. "Look me in the eye and tell me you never saw or spoke to the teenagers that day."

"I don't know what you're getting at."

It was about to be made clear.

"There are several tells people give when they're lying. One of them is avoiding eye contact. With some of my questions, you've looked at me. With others, you looked away. You've also been hedging your statements."

"Hedging my ... what now?"

"When a person is hiding something, to avoid being upfront or truthful, they'll hedge their statements. In this instance, you began your answer to one question by saying 'as far as I recall,' and then the next question I asked, you answered with, 'if you think about it,' both signs you're avoiding whatever it is you'd rather not say."

Danny began tapping the arm of the chair again, but for the first time, his demeanor wasn't a defensive one, which told me I was spot-on.

He was about to crack.

Given Danny's current anxiousness, I asked Giovanni to step outside with Santino. He was reluctant, but he agreed. Once he was out the door, Dorothy leaned forward, her voice soft and low as she addressed her brother. "If you didn't do anything wrong, and you are keeping something to yourself, there's no reason not to tell the truth now. If there's anything you can say to help the detectives on this case, help them put it to rest at long last ... Please, Danny, won't you—"

"There isn't."

I reached into my bag, pulled out an envelope, and walked over to the table. One by one, I pulled photos out, lining them up side by side on the table in front of him. "Brynn Wilson, Aubree Roberts, Aidan Williams, Jackson Nichols, Owen Sherwood, and Cora Callahan, the only one to survive. This is what they looked like before they were attacked. Care to see what they looked like after? I have those photos with me too."

Danny shook his head, his confession unraveling at long last. "I did see ... I saw ... *her*."

15

Danny stabbed a finger over Cora's picture and then swiped his hand across all six photos. They flew off the table, fluttering to the floor. I bent down to scoop them up, placed them back inside my bag, and I sat down next to him.

"What did you mean when you said you saw her?" I asked.

"The day those kids died, I was working on the chair, just like I said," Danny began. "I was planning to sell it the next weekend at the farmers' market. All of that is true."

It just wasn't the *entire* truth.

"What did you leave out of your story?" I asked.

He pressed his hands together. "I used to make furniture out of the wood I found in the area around the cabin. It's the reason I rented the cabin in the first place. It was isolated and quiet, which I also liked. Anyway, I was finishing up the chair, and I realized I didn't have the right size twig to finish the last part along the back."

"Did you leave the cabin to get what you needed?"

"Not at first. It was getting dark out, and I've never liked being outside after dusk. Too easy to get yourself turned around in those woods. But as I stood there, staring at the chair, knowing it was so close to being finished, I just wanted to get it done. I decided if I hurried, I might be able to find what I needed. I grabbed a flashlight, and I headed out."

In his previous statement, Danny had said he'd never left the cabin on the day of the murders, which seemed like an odd thing to lie about. If he was being honest with me now, there was no reason not to tell the police what he'd just told me. It didn't implicate him in anything.

Which meant ... there was something else—something that might implicate him.

"What happened after you left the cabin?" I asked.

"I'd gathered up three good pieces of wood. I figured one of them would get the job done. Problem was, it took me a lot longer to find them than I thought it would. So there was that. Then, when I was headed back to the cabin, I tripped. Thought it was a log at first. The three pieces of wood went flying out of my hands. It wasn't until I stood back up and shined my flashlight that I noticed I hadn't tripped over a log at all. I'd tripped over a woman."

"What did you do next?"

"I bent down and tried shaking her. She didn't stir. Seemed like she'd injured herself, like she'd tripped and maybe hit her head on something and then passed out."

Dorothy joined us at the table and placed her hand on her brother's arm. "Please don't tell me you left the poor girl there."

Danny's breathing began to change.

"Listen, we're not here to judge," I assured him. "You were in a confusing situation. I'm sure it was difficult for you to decide what to do. I just want to know what happened."

He nodded and said, "I shined the flashlight around the area, but there was nothing there, nothing to explain how she ended up on the ground. I turned the light back on her, looking over her body, and I saw blood. She was bleeding from the back of her head, but then I realized, if she'd tripped over something, she would have hit something falling forward. There had to be another explanation."

I was glad he was talking, although he was unnerved about what he'd said so far. If I was going to keep him talking, I needed to be gentle, ease the truth out of him.

"You said she didn't respond," I said.

"Correct."

"Did you know whether she was alive?"

"I tried to ... you know, check her pulse. She didn't have one as far as I could tell. I had no idea who she was or where she'd come from. And I didn't have a phone back then, so there was no one I could even call for help."

"You could have driven into town," Dorothy said.

I wasn't sure what Dorothy hoped to accomplish with her not-so-well-thought-out comments, but all she was doing was pushing Danny to stop talking.

"It would be confusing to know what to do," I said. "I imagine I'd feel the same."

I wouldn't feel the same, but right now, I needed him to feel like I sympathized with the situation he had encountered.

"A minute passed, maybe two, and I decided to leave the girl and figure it all out when I got home," he said. "I walked about twenty feet, and I found another kid. A guy this time. It looked like he'd been whacked in the head a lot harder than the girl had been. Blood was everywhere."

Now we were getting somewhere.

"What else, Danny?"

"I heard something, what sounded like a woman screaming somewhere in the distance. I listened for a minute, but I couldn't figure out what direction it was coming from. I panicked. Someone else was in those woods, someone who was up to no good."

Cora had said that she'd found Jackson right before she was

attacked, leading me to believe they were the two people Danny came across that evening.

As for the screaming he'd heard, that could have come from Brynn or Aubree, in the last moments of their lives.

"After you found a second injured person, what did you do then?" I asked.

Danny hung his hand, shaking it back and forth and saying, "I ran. I ran as fast as I could back to my place. When I got there, I bolted the door, turned all the lights out, and I hid under the stairs all night with an axe in my hand, and my eyes glued to the front door."

"Did you hear or see anything else during the night?"

"Not a thing. Not one thing. It was the quietest night I'd ever had out there. The next morning, I got in my truck, and I drove along the dirt road that led to some of the nearby cabins. I didn't get far before I saw cops had swarmed Millie Callahan's place. I thought they'd figured out what had gone on up there, and I wanted no part of it. I turned right back on around and got the hell out of there."

"Just to be sure, you've never told any of this part of the story to the police before today, right?" I asked.

"Nope."

We all sat in silence for a moment, taking in everything that had been said. Even Dorothy was speechless. Here was her brother who'd found innocent victims of a crime, and for fear of his own life, among other reasons, he left them there.

"I know what you're all thinking," Danny said. "I'm a coward. You think I should have been a hero, done more than I did. When I think back to the screaming I heard, I often wonder if I had the chance to save someone. I don't know. But I could have tried."

"Why didn't you?" Dorothy asked.

"I've thought a lot about it over the years. The fear I felt was stronger than anything I've ever experienced before. I was terrified, worried someone would come after me like they'd gone after them. He was still out there. He could have been anyone."

"So you did nothing," Dorothy said.

Danny bucked out of his chair and jabbed a finger at his sister as he shouted, "Shut up! Just shut up! You have no idea what you're going to do in a situation like that until you're in it. Besides, it's not like I saw anything that would have made a difference. If I had, it would be different."

"Why tell me all of this now?" I asked.

He paused a moment, then said, "It's not easy keeping something like this in for as long as I have. It's taken a heavy toll. When I realized Cora was alive when I found her, and the guilt I've endured over that fact alone is almost too painful to bear."

I thought back to the panicked look in his eyes when he'd opened the door and Dorothy explained who I was and why I was there.

"The way you reacted when I started questioning you earlier makes a lot more sense to me," I said.

"Think about it. The case had gone cold, and I thought it would stay that way. Then you show up here with your questions, and I learn the case has been reopened."

"And forensic evidence has come a long way since then."

He pointed at me and said, "You got it. What if I left something behind when I tripped over Cora. A hair, or I don't know ... anything. I don't see how I could have, but there's this little part of me that's saying, 'What if you did?'"

Being at the crime scene right after the murders happened made him a viable suspect. If it turned out Silas was able to place him there through a piece of old evidence brought in for reexamination, I understood why Danny wanted to get out of town.

"I meant what I said before, about not pressing charges," I said.

Danny looked at Giovanni and then me. "I'm sorry. I never meant to hurt you."

"You need to go down to the police station and tell them what you just told me."

"What are they going to do when they find out I lied?"

Good question.

I supposed it depended on what they thought when he gave them a new statement, and whether they chose to believe it. "I don't know," I said. "I'll go to the department with you and talk with Chief Foley. I'll go over the conversation we had today, and I won't mention the part about you pepper-spraying me in the face."

Not yet, anyway.

"Why would you leave it out?" Danny asked. "You don't even know me."

"I gave you my word. I need to ask ... is there anything more, anything you haven't said?"

"No, you know everything now."

"Good."

I rose from my seat, blinking a few times to relubricate my eyes, which hadn't stopped stinging all the way yet.

"Wait," Danny said, and I turned back to him.

"What is it?"

"What if I tell them everything I just told you and they don't believe me? What if they think I lied then and I'm lying now?"

"I know it's hard, Danny," I said. "But have a little faith in the justice system, and believe me when I say they're not interested in catching the wrong guy. They're interested in catching the right guy, and if the right guy isn't you, there's no need to worry. Now, I'm done here."

And with that, I walked out the door.

16

I was sitting in Foley's office, waiting for Whitlock to finish questioning Danny. Foley was sitting across from me, his brow raised as he said, "What's going on with your eyes? They're all red."

"I've been rubbing them—a lot," I said.

It was the truth.

I *had* been rubbing them a lot.

It just wasn't the whole truth.

"I don't know if you've looked in the mirror much today, but it looks like you're developing some sort of infection," he said. "Might want to think about getting it looked at."

"If the redness doesn't go away, I will."

Foley looked past me at Giovanni, who was sitting out in the hall, chatting with Dorothy. She'd insisted on coming along as a show of support for her brother.

"You ... ehh, decide you want a little company today?" Foley asked.

Until now, I hadn't given any thought to how I would explain Giovanni's presence.

"He ... ahh, didn't have anything going on today, so I thought I'd bring him along."

Foley stared at me for a moment.

It was obvious he didn't believe me, but I wouldn't be offering any further explanation.

He laced his hands together on top of his desk and said, "So, what's with the guy you just brought in? What's his story?"

"Danny rented and lived in a cabin close to where the teens were killed. He was questioned back then, but today I found out he omitted a few things from the story he originally told police."

"Why?"

"He's the type of person who thinks everyone has it out for him. And given he doesn't have much faith in law enforcement, he says he was scared to tell the truth."

"What *is* the truth?"

"In Danny's original statement, he said he'd never seen any of the teens before, but he had. The night they were murdered, he was in the forest. It was getting dark, and as he was heading back to his cabin, he tripped over Cora's body. He claims he thought she was dead. He walked a little farther and found one of the boys. I believe it was Jackson."

"And Danny didn't report any of it?"

I shook my head. "He went back to his cabin, locked the door, and spent the night worrying a madman was going around murdering people in the area, and he was next."

"A madman *was* going around murdering people in his area. Seems a bit strange to withhold something as big as that, whether you're a fan of the law or not."

"According to him, he thought the cops would find a way to convict him for the murders if he spoke up. He said it wasn't unusual for innocent people to be incarcerated, and he didn't want to be one of those cases."

Foley bounced a pencil off his desk, thinking. "Why tell the truth now?"

"Let's just say I was good at convincing him it was the right thing to do."

"What do you think about his new story? You think he's being honest, or is the guy still lying?"

"I believe he came across the teens like he said. Beyond that, I don't know what to think. After he admitted the truth, he seemed relieved to get it off his chest after all this time. Doesn't mean he's innocent though."

"Right. No matter how you look at it, he withheld evidence, he lied to the police. He broke the law. We could still charge him."

"I know. You don't *have* to charge him though. Not yet. Right?"

Foley raised a brow. "Why do you care?"

"I don't know. I shouldn't, but I do. The point is for us to solve the case. His information might help. I guess there's something to be said for his confession, even if it is a little late."

"A *little*? I wouldn't call two decades a little anything. Maybe an honest confession back then wouldn't have made a difference in the case, but what if it had?"

"I don't see how it would have changed anything. I could be wrong. Have you spoken to my mother today?"

His eyes narrowed. "I see what you're doing."

I was changing the subject, because if I didn't, I got the impression we would go 'round and 'round about Danny, and I didn't see the point.

"Well, have you?" I pressed.

"I don't have any interest in discussing Darlene right now, or her ridiculous expectations."

"Whitlock and Harvey came to see me last night to let me know they're planning to work the case together. I noticed Harvey isn't around, though."

"No, he is not. If Whitlock wants to run around town with Harvey on his own time, fine. I understand Harvey's investment in this case, but he's retired. He doesn't belong here at the department, questioning people."

I was disappointed.

I thought Foley would have been more open to the idea of allowing them to work together. Harvey wasn't asking to help investigate just any murder. He was asking to investigate an old case—one where he had a lot of skin in the game.

"Have you told Harvey how you feel?" I asked.

"I have, and he understands. It's your mother who's taking issue with my decision. It's one thing to have Harvey step in and assist Whitlock. It's another to have your mother think it's all right to insert herself where she doesn't belong."

"You have to admit, it is a bit funny to think of those three driving around town, trying to solve the murders."

Foley shook his head and said, "Oh, I have thought about it. Had a good laugh as soon as Whitlock informed me of their ridiculous plan."

"Who knows? Maybe they'll surprise us all. Perhaps you should reconsider your position."

"Noted. What do you have going on for the rest of the day?"

"Cora gave me a key to her grandmother's cabin. I'm going to drive out and have a look around. She said they haven't been out there since the murders took place. I have no idea what to expect, but I'm up for anything. I'm just hoping something will come of it."

17

Before leaving the police department, I'd pulled Whitlock to the side to discuss his interview with Danny. Whitlock expressed disappointment that Danny had changed his story, but he was glad to hear what we hoped was the truth this time around. Then he excused himself so he could relay the details of the interview to Foley, who was in two minds about how to handle Danny.

As Giovanni and I drove up to the cabin, Whitlock called to inform me they'd agreed not to charge Danny but gave him strict instructions *not* to leave town.

The winding road to the crime scene offered frequent scenic views of the surrounding area. The sun had just begun its descent, dipping behind the mountains as it offered a soft glow to the start of the evening.

We pulled up to the cabin, and I sat for a moment with the window open, taking in the tranquility—a sharp contrast to what had happened here all those years ago.

When we stepped out of the car, Giovanni stayed in the background, understanding my need to immerse myself in the here and now—and even more important—to the there and then.

In the distance, birds chirped and crickets began their nightly songs. The cabin was surrounded by a variety of trees—oaks, redwoods, and pines, each offering a picturesque, peaceful feeling—a feeling like nothing bad had ever happened there, even though it had.

I took in a lungful of fresh forest air and turned toward Giovanni.

"It's so calm and tranquil," I said. "And yet, I can almost feel their spirits all around me."

Giovanni raised a finger and said, "If you don't seek death, you won't die."

"What?"

"It's a Chinese proverb. I've always taken it to mean if you don't seek out trouble, trouble won't find you. Thinking about what took place here, I'm not sure I believe it to be true. They came here to celebrate life, an end of an era following high school graduation and the beginning of a new, bright future. They didn't invite death. Death invited itself."

I wanted to believe he was right, that they were, in fact, innocent. I wanted to believe they hadn't brought their own deaths on themselves in some way.

My thoughts turned toward Xander. Earlier, Hunter had texted me his home address. He still lived in Cambria. I planned on paying him a visit in the morning.

I wondered what he'd have to say about his old classmates.

After all this time, what did he think of them now?

Giovanni wrapped his arm around me. "What would you like to do first?"

I retrieved the case file I'd set on the passenger seat, flipping it open and searching through the pages until I came to the one I was looking for—a handwritten map showing the exact location where the teens were found.

"We're losing daylight," I said. "I figure we have a little over an hour to look around. I'd like to go to the places where Aidan, Jackson, and Owen were found."

Giovanni looked at the map. The areas the teens were found had been circled. Owen was the closest to the cabin, less than twenty feet away from the cabin's front steps, which made sense. He'd gone out to his car to retrieve something, a task that should have taken him no more than a minute or two.

"Owen was the first one to be attacked," I said. "I believe it happened right after he opened the car door. According to the police report, blood was found inside the car on the driver's seat, and there was also a bloody fingerprint on the window. Both the blood from the seat and the fingerprint were a match to Owen. But he didn't die here at the car, where he was assaulted."

"What do you mean?"

"Owen was struck twice. The police report states there were distinct dirt marks leading to the side of the cabin, a side that has no windows. Owen must have been dragged there from the car. I assume it's because the killer wanted to get him out of the way to a place where he couldn't be seen from the cabin's front windows."

I walked to the area where the police had found Owen. There wasn't much to see. Twenty years ago, there had been a flower garden on this side of the house. Now it was overgrown with weeds. All that remained of the garden were a few empty terra cotta pots and a rusted, red wheelbarrow, which was tipped on its side.

"It's so different now than it was in the pictures I've seen," I said.

"Time changes everything."

Indeed.

I glanced back at the map. "Next up is Jackson."

I pivoted, heading in the opposite direction. Giovanni followed. We hadn't made it far when I stopped.

"I'm not sure I'm leading us to the right spot," I said.

"Let me have a look at the map," Giovanni said.

I handed it to him. While he looked it over, I cupped a hand over my forehead like a visor, turning all the way around as I looked for clues as to where we'd find the place the police had found Jackson.

I grabbed Giovanni's arm. "Wait a minute. I see what looks like a memorial of some kind. Over there."

I took off toward a large wooden cross that had been nailed to a tree. Once painted white, the harsh winter weather had not been kind, picking away at the wood-grain layers of the cross, which caused it to split and peel.

In front of the cross, a variety of fake flowers had been stuck into the ground. They, too, looked old, as did all the other trinkets that had been left there, save for one thing—a football. It was in pristine condition.

Giovanni joined me, bending down to examine the mementos that had been placed to honor young Jackson's life. Weathered photos, a football jersey bearing his number, and a beaded necklace in the school colors, among other things.

"The cabin may not have been occupied all these years, but someone's been out here," he said.

"I'm assuming it's Jackson's family."

"The football's new."

"I thought the same thing," I said. "This month marks the twentieth anniversary of their deaths. Maybe someone from his family brought the football in remembrance."

Giovanni glanced at the cross and then turned toward the cabin. "How far was Jackson from the third kid they found?"

"Aidan was discovered fifteen feet away from here. If it wasn't dark at the time Cora found Jackson, I'm sure she would have also seen Aidan. She said as much. In the notes from the case file, Harvey mentioned they thought Aidan might have put up a fight against his attacker. It leads me to believe Jackson was attacked first, but he was unsuccessful. It's a miracle Cora made it out alive."

"She's a lucky woman."

I wasn't so sure Cora would agree.

"Aidan was the only victim to have skin under his fingernails, hence the reason they think he'd fought back," I said. "Skin cells can get trapped beneath fingernails, so scrapings were taken and tested with the available DNA technology at the time. None of the testing went anywhere, though."

"It's possible the killer wasn't in the criminal database twenty years ago, but perhaps he is now."

I was hopeful he might be.

"I need to talk to Silas," I said. "But I imagine it's going to be a while before he has any test results."

I looked around.

Darkness was fast approaching, and with it, the visibility was all but gone.

"Let's head back to the cabin," I said. "Since Cora's family abandoned this place, I imagine there won't be any electricity. Good thing we brought our own source of light."

I'd had enough foresight to put a work light that attached to a tripod in the car when I left the office that morning. I'd also grabbed a couple of high-powered flashlights.

We trekked back to the car, removing what we needed, and made our way up the cabin steps.

I reached in my pocket to pull out the key Cora had given me, but Giovanni stopped me, saying, "We don't need it. The door is open."

I looked at where he was pointing. The door was a couple of inches ajar.

"Huh," I said. "How strange."

I used my foot to ease the door open. The tripod with the work light was in my left hand, and a flashlight in the right. I set the tripod down and turned both lights on.

Looking around, the first thing I noticed was the dust. Every inch of the cabin was caked in it. Old furniture was scattered around, none of it covered or preserved in any way. We'd stepped back into a place that had been frozen in time, a place full of memories, including the last few moments of the teens' lives.

"The dust is so thick, and the air is stale, I'm finding it hard to breathe," I said. "I wish we'd come earlier in the day. If there is something to see here, I'm worried I won't see it."

"We can always return tomorrow."

I didn't want to make the drive again tomorrow, but if I had to, I would.

"Let's do a quick walkthrough, and then we'll leave," I said.

We made our way through the kitchen, crossed the dining room, and entered the living room, where the bloodstains from Brynn and Aubree's murders were still visible. Standing there was surreal. I thought about how scared they must have been and how alone they must have felt at the end.

A stereo sat on the fireplace mantel. Next to it was a stack of CDs—50 Cent, Avril Lavigne, Eminem, and Toby Keith, among others.

"How are you doing?" Giovanni asked.

"It's always hard to witness the place where someone died. My feelings are all over the place. I can imagine the excitement they all felt when they first arrived, oblivious of what was to come. It's a shame. They were all too young to have their lives stripped away at the hands of a psycho."

A wave of emotion came over me, and I swallowed hard, pushing it down. I was here to do a job. What I needed now was to focus.

"Let's head upstairs," I said. "I had a chance to take a look at Cora's initial statement on the way here. She detailed who stayed in what room."

We focused our flashlights on the stairs and made our ascent.

The first room we entered was Owen's. A coat and a pair of socks were sitting on the bed. Hiking boots on the floor. In the ensuite bathroom, I found a pack of gum, a comb, and men's hair gel. Signs of life in a place that had seen too much death.

We moved across the hall, entering the room Brynn and Aidan had stayed in. It, too, appeared to have remained untouched. Aside from the unmade bed, there were no signs of Brynn and Aidan ever being there. Whatever they had with them that day, it wasn't here any longer.

I skipped over Aubree and Jackson's room and focused on the grandmother's room, the same room Cora had locked herself in while waiting for the police.

The door squeaked as I pushed it opened.

I steadied my flashlight, peered into the room, and gasped.

"What is it?" Giovanni asked. "What do you see?"

I moved the flashlight from left to right and clarity came in the form of words written on the wall in thick red marker:

>WELCOME BACK, CORA
>GONE BUT NOT FORGOTTEN

18

I yanked my phone out of my pocket, desperate to make a call, but I had no cell service. Giovanni didn't either.

"We need to get out of here and get back to town," I said.

"You're worried about Cora," he said.

I nodded.

"The first thing I thought when I saw the writing on the wall was how much I wanted it to be a prank," I said. "I figured it could have been the work of a bunch of high school kids who heard about this place and think it's haunted. You know how rumors go."

"All too well."

"My instinct tells me it wasn't, though."

"You think the killer knows Cora is back in town."

"I do, and it makes me think he's close by. Close enough to keep tabs on what's going on around here. Cora and her family need to be made aware of what we found."

Giovanni agreed, and we raced downstairs, blowing past the tripod without stopping to grab it. There was something much more important we needed to be holding right now—our guns.

We headed back to town, my eyes making frequent contact with my phone to see if I had service yet. Six excruciating minutes later, I did, and I gave Cora a call. It rang several times and went to voicemail.

"No luck?" Giovanni asked.

"She's not answering."

I drummed my fingers along the armrest, trying to decide what to do next, and then I got an idea. I called Aunt Laura. Given she was friends with Cora's mother, Ginger, I figured she could give me her number.

The phone rang once ...

Twice ...

Three times ...

And then, "Hello, kiddo. How's your day been?"

"I ... uhh ... it's been crazy."

"You sound like you're out of breath. Is everything okay?"

"No, it's not."

"Care to talk about it?"

Not right now.

I had more pressing matters on my mind.

"I'm in the car with Giovanni," I said. "We just came from Millie Callahan's cabin. I've been trying to reach Cora, and she's not answering her phone. Can you give me her mother's number?"

"She's not home right now. She's at the grocery store. But you're in luck. I'm already at their house, waiting for Ginger to return. I made dinner for them tonight. Anyway, Cora's car is in the driveway, though. I haven't talked to her yet, but I'm guessing she's in her room. I'll walk down the hall and see, and then I can give you the phone, so you can talk to her. Hold on a second."

I heard the sound of footsteps shuffling down the hall.

There was a knock, and then, "Cora, dear. It's Laura. I have Georgiana on the phone. She'd like to speak with you."

I waited.

It was quiet for a moment, and then Aunt Laura said, "How odd."

"What's odd?" I asked.

"Cora hasn't acknowledged me, and she's not coming to the door. What would you like me to do?"

The uneasiness stirring inside me was growing worse.

"Don't wait for her to come to the door," I said. "Check and see if she's in her room."

"She might be asleep. How about I check the rest of the house first before I enter her room without permission, though?"

"All right."

A few minutes passed, and there was no sign of Cora.

"I'm heading back to her room now," Aunt Laura said. "Care to tell me what on earth is going on?"

I took a deep breath in and said, "When we were at the cabin, we saw an ominous message written in red marker on Millie's bedroom wall. I believe the person responsible for the murders twenty years ago knows Cora is back in town."

"Oh, dear. I'm entering her room as we speak."

A door was opened, and Aunt Laura said, "Cora, are you here?"

"Is she there?"

"I don't think so. Let me check the bathroom."

After a brief pause, Aunt Laura said, "She's not in the bathroom either. It doesn't make sense. She didn't go with Ginger to the store, and like I said, her car is in the driveway, so …"

"Look around the bedroom. Tell me what you see."

"Let's see … I've just walked over to her bed. There's an open yearbook on top of Cora's pillow, and, oh, even more strange. Her cell phone is here. I can't imagine Cora leaving home without it."

There was a loud gasp, and I said, "What is it? What's happening?"

"The window's open, which wouldn't alarm me, except the screen is missing. I'm sorry to say I don't know where Cora is, Gigi. But I can tell you one thing for certain—she's not here."

19

As Giovanni and I pulled to a stop in front of the Callahans' house, I identified a few cars parked outside: Foley's truck, Whitlock's car, and a patrol car. We rushed to the front door, and as we walked inside, Whitlock was there waiting for me.

"I ... we got here as fast as we could," I said. "Have you heard anything from Cora? Do you know what's going on?"

Whitlock placed a hand on my shoulder. "We haven't heard from her. Why don't you take a breath? Looks like you need it."

I did.

I pressed a hand to my chest, feeling the quickened pace of my heartbeat. I closed my eyes, focusing on my breathing. What happened in the past couldn't be changed, and I was no use to Cora if I couldn't keep my anxiety in check. My focus belonged in the present.

I reopened my eyes, and Whitlock said, "Feel better?"

"A little," I said. "What can you tell me?"

"Not much. There is one thing, though. There's a note tucked beneath one of the windshield wipers on Cora's car. Said something like: 'Welcome back. Gone but not forgotten.'"

The same words written on Millie's bedroom wall.

"We've been through the house, inside and out," Whitlock said. "Officers Higgins and Decker are canvassing the area, knocking on doors. Other than the note, there's no other information to report."

"I don't even want to think about what may have happened to her. After what Cora's been through, to come back to town all these years later only to relive her worst nightmare ... it's—"

"Hey, I understand how you feel, but there's no use jumping to conclusions until we have a better idea of what happened here. Silas is on his way to dust her room, the window, and the area around it for prints."

Down the hall, I heard my name being called.

Whitlock and I followed the voice to Cora's bedroom, where Foley was waiting.

He pointed at me and said, "Before you say anything, we're doing everything we can to locate her."

"I know you are. It's my fault. I feel like I've failed her. I was supposed to keep her safe. I shouldn't have assumed she would be."

"Look, this isn't about fault. No one's to blame. It's been a long time. None of us had any way of knowing the perpetrator might still be in the area, let alone if he was still alive."

I threw my hands into the air, saying, "Well, we know now."

"Let's concentrate our efforts on the facts. Getting all worked up isn't going to bring her home safely. Right now, our sole focus is on making a plan and finding her."

Finding her *before* it was too late ... *if* it wasn't already.

Thoughts flashed through my mind ...

Cora dead in a ditch somewhere.

Cora being captured and tortured.

No matter what direction my thoughts went in, it wasn't good.

"I was supposed to be the person she could rely on," I said. "When she came to see me, she said it was the first time in a long time that she felt like she could see a future for herself, a future where she could put the past behind her."

"You couldn't have known the murderer was still out there until you saw the message left at the cabin," Foley said. "There's been no other contact since the murders took place."

Somewhere inside the house, I heard a wailing sound, the sound of a woman in turmoil.

"I imagine Ginger isn't taking this well," I said.

Whitlock and Foley exchanged worried glances.

"She is not," Whitlock said. "I've tried to question her about Cora's comings and goings today, but she's not interested in talking to us. Your aunt is with her now, and she knows we need our questions answered. We're hoping she might get somewhere."

I didn't blame Ginger for not feeling like talking to the police.

At this point, I was sure she felt let down by all of us.

"Let's get back to doing what we do best, shall we," Foley said.

I reached in my pocket, took out my phone, and pulled up a photo. "This is a bit dark, but I thought you'd want a visual of the writing on the wall at the cabin. Guess it's the same message that was left on Cora's car."

I turned my phone around, and Foley and Whitlock bent down to take a closer look. In unison, they repeated the phrase left on Millie's bedroom wall.

"Yep, same exact words," Foley said.

"Everything in the cabin looked like it hadn't been touched in twenty years," I said. "Except for this writing. It looked fresh, like the message had just been written on the wall."

"Is there any electricity inside the cabin?"

I shook my head. "We were out there at dusk, and we had to use flashlights to look around."

"I'll have Whitlock stop by there tomorrow."

In the distance, I heard, "Yoohoo, where is everyone?"

Foley rolled his eyes and said, "I don't think I have it in me to deal with your mother right now."

"Let me see if I can cut her off at the pass," I said.

Foley placed a hand on my arm and said, "I appreciate you. More than you know."

I found Harvey and my mother in the living room, standing beside Giovanni.

"Can someone please tell me what is going on?" my mother huffed. "We're supposed to be part of this investigation, and no one is telling us anything. Well, that is to say, Whitlock reached out to Harvey to say Cora is missing. What I want to know is, how did this happen?"

My mother *wasn't* part of the investigation, no matter how much she wanted to be—a fact I had no intention of arguing with her about now. I didn't want to discuss what we'd seen at the cabin either, but I assumed she already knew, which meant there wasn't any way around it. If she didn't hear it from me, she'd hear it from someone else.

"Earlier, at Millie's cabin, I discovered someone had left a message on the wall," I said. "The same message was on a note found on Cora's car."

My mother turned toward me. "Yes, yes, I heard. When you say a message, what do you mean, a threat?"

"Yes."

"Well, don't keep us in suspense. What did it say?"

I told her.

"As soon as I read the message, I tried to get in touch with Cora, and then I learned she was missing," I said.

"Missing for how long?"

"I don't know. Whitlock tried speaking to Ginger about what Cora's been up to today. She wasn't in the mood to talk."

My mother slid her handbag off her shoulder, handed it to Harvey, and rolled up her sleeves. "Where is she? Give me five minutes with the woman. I'll have her singing like a lark."

I shook my head. "You can't. She's in her bedroom with Aunt Laura right now, and she's not doing well. The last thing she needs is to be questioned. I'm not saying she won't be. I'm saying she isn't ready yet, and we need to respect that. The more we show her some respect, the better chance we have of her telling us what she knows."

"Time is wasting, Georgiana. You know that better than anyone."

"I do. I also know Aunt Laura, and she's aware of what we want to know. Let's give her a chance to see if she can get Ginger to open up."

My mother crossed her arms and said, "How long do you expect us to wait? Doesn't Ginger understand we have questions because we're trying to help?"

Harvey cut in, no doubt attempting to alleviate my mother's concerns. "Let's give Laura a chance at least."

His attempt to calm my mother down did not go as expected.

"If we're of no use here, then why are we here?" my mother stated. "I don't see the point."

Giovanni, who had a talent of getting through to my mother in a way no one else could, took his turn at calming her.

"Darlene, I was thinking of going for a drive. There's nothing to do here. Not right now. If you care to join me, I'll tell you all about our visit to the cabin today. I think you'll find it fascinating."

In truth, *fascinating* wasn't anywhere near the right word to describe what we'd seen. But I hoped his suggestion worked.

My mother shot me a look, then Harvey, back to Giovanni. "I would love to join you. Thank you, Giovanni, for making me feel like a part of it all. No one else seems to care."

I let the passive-aggressive comment slide and said nothing.

She took back her purse from Harvey and turned, leaving the room without saying another word. Giovanni planted a kiss on my forehead, and I wrapped my arms around him, whispering, "Thank you."

Once they were outside, Harvey took a seat on the couch, leaning back like he wanted to melt into it.

"I need your advice, Georgiana," he said.

"Of course. How can I help?"

"I don't know what to do. Your mother ... she's becoming too involved. Makes me want to step back, let you and Whitlock finish the investigation. If we keep going like this, I'm not sure I can handle it."

"Do you want to take a step back?"

"I don't. It's just ... ever since she offered her 'help,' my blood pressure has gone way up."

"Is she aware?"

He scoffed. "Not a bit. She thinks being involved in the case will somehow help me. It's not. It's making things worse."

"Have you tried talking to her about it?"

"Not yet. I'm not sure how she'll take it."

"It's worth a conversation. You know how important your health is to her, and she respects honesty, even if it's hard for her to take."

"Working on this case again is exciting. I have a good feeling about it, a feeling like we're going to solve it this time. I thought we could do it together, but now, I don't see how we can."

There had to be a way to make it all work—a way for Harvey to take a step back but still feel involved, while at the same time, encouraging my mother to let Harvey and Whitlock investigate on their own.

Then, it came to me.

"I have an idea," I said.

"Wonderful."

"What if we kept you in the loop through text messages? You'd know everything going on, and you could message us when you have something to add."

He rubbed his hands together and said, "Hmm, could work. It's worth a try, I suppose. Anything to get Darlene back to her regular schedule. She's been all over me, and we're just getting started."

"It's settled, then."

I was about to suggest we check in on Foley and Whitlock before my mother returned when I heard the front door open.

"They couldn't be back so soon," Harvey said. "Could they?"

"No, Giovanni will keep her out as long as he can. I bet it's Silas. He was on his way over to dust for prints."

I looked up, expecting to see Silas walk into the room and slapped a hand against my mouth, blinking once and then a second time to be sure what I was witnessing was real.

"Cora?" I said. "Where have you been?"

She raised a brow, as if confused. "Hey, guys. What's with all the cars parked outside? Is something going on?"

20

What followed after everyone learned Cora was safe was a joyous reunion between mother and daughter, a mother whose biggest fear had been that her daughter had been abducted by the Cabin Killer.

As we gathered around to celebrate Cora's return, my mind was brimming with unanswered questions:

Where had Cora been all this time?
Why had she left the house without her cell phone?
Why was the screen missing from her bedroom window?

I needed answers to make everything make sense.

And right now, it didn't.

As much as I wanted to question Cora, I shelved my curiosity, deciding I'd wait until everything calmed down, and I was able to speak to her alone.

Time passed, and one by one, those who'd gathered at Ginger's house began to leave.

As Foley made his exit, he told Ginger he'd assign officers to sit across the street in a patrol car in shifts for as long as it was needed. It came as a welcome relief. Ginger and Cora would sleep better knowing they were being looked after.

Aunt Laura said her goodbyes, and a few minutes later, Ginger retired to bed, leaving Cora and I alone to talk.

"I don't know about you, but after what just happened, I could use a glass of wine," Cora said. "Care to join me?"

I nodded, and we walked to the kitchen. Cora removed a couple of glasses from the cabinet and poured a pinot noir into each.

I slid onto a barstool, and Cora set a glass in front of me and said, "I'm sorry for making everyone worry. I had no idea leaving the house would cause so many problems."

"You have nothing to be sorry about. You're safe. Nothing else matters."

"I didn't realize how much trouble it would cause if I didn't tell you my plans. I was focused on how much I needed a moment to myself. I promise not to leave the house again without taking my cell phone with me."

"How are you feeling about the note left on your car?"

"When Chief Foley mentioned it after I got home, part of me wanted to leave. The other part of me is tired of running from my past. If I run, the killer wins, *again*. He doesn't get to win ... not this time."

Cora was taking a stand.

I was impressed.

"I heard you talking to Whitlock earlier," I said. "But I only caught bits and pieces of the conversation. I have so many questions."

"Ask me anything."

"Why did you leave?"

Cora took a sip of her wine and said, "I was in my room earlier, looking through the yearbook again. I came across a photo of the six of us, and I started to feel overwhelmed."

"Is that why you decided to leave the house?"

"Yeah, I needed to clear my head and get away from it all for a minute. Between the new investigation and my father's illness, it's been a lot to take in, you know?"

"I do. Why did you leave your phone behind?"

"I wanted to be alone with my thoughts. When I left, I didn't plan on being gone long. I lost track of time."

"Do you feel better now?"

Cora nodded. "A lot better. As I walked through the neighborhood, I realized how much I've missed this town. Sure, it holds a lot of bad memories, but it also holds some of my best ones too."

"Where did you go?"

"There's a park about a mile from here. When Owen was alive, we'd walk over to it sometimes to hang out, catch up on things. I always thought of the park as 'our place,' and I realized I hadn't been back there since he died."

"How did it feel to be there again?"

"A lot more comfortable than I thought it would be. Before I left the house, I started thinking about a place I could go where I knew I'd feel a sense of peace. I was looking at a photo of Owen, and I wished I could talk to him again. A memory came back about a time we were at the park together, and I realized it was the one place I connected to him most."

"Did you feel connected to him when you were there just now?"

"In a way ... I, I'm sure you'll think I'm crazy for admitting this, but I talked to him tonight. I sat on the same park bench we used to sit on together, and I spoke to him as though he was sitting right next to me."

"I don't think it sounds crazy at all," I said. "You miss him in the same way I miss my daughter."

"You have a daughter?"

"I *had* a daughter. She died when she was a toddler, and we buried her next to my father. I visit their graves every week, and I talk to them both."

Cora took another sip of wine and said, "What do you think happens after we die? Do you think the spirits of those we love are still around, watching over us and what becomes of our lives?"

"I want to believe they are. If not all the time, when we need them most. I believe we're all connected—the living and the dead."

"Can I confess something to you?"

"Sure."

"As I was leaving the park tonight, I told Owen I loved him. I said I'd always loved him. I also said I was sorry he was taken before we had the chance to start our love story together."

"What you said ... it's beautiful."

We sat for a time, enjoying the wine, and unwinding from the heaviness of the day. Given the knowledge the killer had reached out to her in a personal way, I was impressed with how she was handling it. The nervousness she'd had the day before was gone. For now, at least.

"I have another question for you," I said. "What happened to the screen on your window?"

"The cops wondered the same thing. This morning, a bird smacked right into the window with such force, it dented some of the metal around the screen. I removed the screen and put it in the trunk of my car. I was going to drive to the hardware store and get it replaced, but the day got away from me."

"Is the bird okay?"

"Oh, yeah. I went out to check on the little guy. He was sitting on the grass. I thought he'd hurt himself, but I think he was just stunned. After a couple of minutes, he flapped his wings and flew away like nothing had ever happened."

"I'm a big fan of birds," I said. "It makes me a nerd, I suppose, but I don't care. Something about watching them brings me peace."

"Have you always been into birds?"

I smiled and said, "Ever since my father died. I haven't told many people this, but sometimes when I think of him, a bird appears and just hovers around, not close enough for me to touch, but close enough."

"Is it the same kind of bird every time or ...?"

"Different birds, but the behavior is the same."

Cora reached for the bottle of wine and turned toward me. "Want a refill?"

"I'm all right. I should head out soon. But you go right ahead."

She shrugged, poured a second glass for herself, and then sat there, staring at it. Something was bothering her.

"Are you all right?" I asked.

"There's so much going through my mind right now."

"Care to share? I'm a good listener."

"When I found out about the message left at the cabin and on my car window, I wanted to believe it was a joke, you know? I wanted to believe he's not around here, that he doesn't care about what happened to me anymore. I wanted to believe someone else wrote it—not him. Do you think it's possible?"

It was a question I'd been debating myself.

"My gut says yes, he wrote it," I said.

Cora bit down on her lip, going quiet for a time.

"I'm a lot stronger of a person now than I was in the past," she said. "I also know my way around a gun. There's strength in that."

"Is the writing on the wall and in the note the only thing that's bothering you, or is there something else?"

"I ... I want to talk to you about someone. I'll be right back."

Cora left the room, returning with the yearbook in hand.

She set it down in front of me on the kitchen counter and flipped it open, thumbing through pages until she got to the one she wanted. "It's amazing the things I've remembered as I've looked through some of this book."

"What stood out to you the most?"

She pressed a finger against a black-and-white photo and said, "*Him*."

I squinted, taking a good look at the boy in question. He was dressed in faded jeans and a white long-sleeved shirt with a gray T-shirt over it.

"Who is he?" I asked.

"His name is Ty Conroy. He was in our graduating class. His father was our biology teacher."

"How well did you know him?"

"Not as well as Jackson did. Toward the end of the school year, Jackson started stressing out about not passing the final biology exam. Jackson's stepdad was ... ahh, let's just say he was always hard on Jackson, and not just when it came to his grades."

"Hard in what way?"

"I never saw any signs Jackson was being abused, you know, in a physical way, but Aubree did. She saw bruises on one of his shoulders and back."

"Did Aubree ask him about it?"

"Yeah. As soon as she did, Jackson changed the subject. She thought he was upset with her for asking, so I don't think she ever brought it up again."

If Jackson's stepfather was abusing him, the fact Jackson had been known to be a bully at school made a lot more sense to me now.

His stepfather took out his anger on Jackson.

Jackson, in turn, took his anger out on someone else—someone he could vent his frustration on—instead of venting it on his stepfather.

"What do you know about Jackson's stepdad?" I asked.

"I saw him a few times at football games. He was a big guy, a lot bigger than Jackson. Everything about him gave off bad vibes."

"In what way?"

Cora paused a moment, like she was thinking about how to describe him to me.

"He always seemed ... well, mean," she said. "If Jackson was being abused, I doubt his mother knew. Back then she was working a lot at the family business."

"And the stepdad, what did he do for a job?"

"From the stuff Jackson told us about him, it sounded like before his stepdad got together with his mom, he was always in between jobs, or getting fired from a job not long after starting it. Once he met Jackson's mom, he started working for the family business too."

"What type of business?"

"A car dealership."

I glanced back at the photo of Ty, wondering what the connection was between Ty and Jackson. There must have been one. Why else would Cora have shown me a photo of him and then start talking about Jackson?

"I'm assuming the story you just told me about Jackson's stepdad relates to Ty in some way," I said.

Cora nodded. "Ty was the type of person who'd do anything to hang out with guys like Jackson. About a week before final exams, Jackson told Ty he was worried he wasn't going to pass his biology test. If his final grade wasn't an A or a B, his stepdad threatened not to allow Jackson access to the funds his mother had set aside for him for college."

"Did he get a good grade?"

"He did, but it wasn't because he studied hard for the test. Ty gave Jackson a copy of his dad's test a few days before the exam. I guess Ty's dad had used the same final exam for years."

"Aside from Jackson, did anyone else see the test before the exam?"

Cora hung her head and said, "Yes. A couple of nights before the exam, we were all hanging out in my backyard, talking about the camping trip. Jackson told me about the test, and then he passed it around. At the time, I remember thinking it was too good to be true. I didn't believe it was the actual test."

"Was it?"

"Yeah, word for word. I'll never forget the day we took the exam. We were all looking around at each other, shocked. Thing is, when Ty gave Jackson a copy of the test, he made Jackson promise not to show it to anyone else."

"And Jackson broke his promise by showing it to all of you. How many of you saw the test?"

Cora looked to the side, thinking. "Jackson, Aidan, Brynn, Aubree, *me*."

"What about Owen?"

"He refused to look at it. He said he was uncomfortable about it and would rather take his chances. But he was always a whiz in school, a straight-A student. He didn't need to look at it."

"And you?"

"I only saw the first page of the test before the actual exam. As I was looking at it, I realized the questions were in line with what we'd learned that year. It made me feel weird. I knew it was wrong, so after I looked over the first several questions, I handed the test back to Jackson."

I leaned forward, crossing my arms over the kitchen counter. "Did anyone ever find out they cheated?"

"Yep, the day after the test, Jackson, Aidan, Brynn, and Aubree were called into the principal's office. Ty's dad was there, and he told the principal he thought the four of them had cheated. They all scored one hundred percent on the test, which was stupid of them to do. It made the fact they'd cheated obvious."

"Did Ty's dad know how they'd cheated?"

"Not at first, and they didn't admit it either, not until their parents were called."

"What happened then?" I asked.

"When Jackson's stepdad showed up, he outed all of them. He said he remembered seeing a copy of the test in Jackson's bedroom. His stepdad thought it was a practice test at the time, something to help the students get ready for the real test."

"After Jackson's stepdad admitted to seeing the test, did they admit they'd cheated?"

"Not while they were in the principal's office. The next day, when the principal got to his office, there was an anonymous note stuck in the doorjamb. The note revealed Ty had been the one to share the answers to his father's test with Jackson."

It was a sad story.

All Ty wanted was to be accepted, just like Xander.

It was possible he thought helping Jackson would somehow create a friendship between them. I doubted it would have, whether the truth of what he'd done came out or not.

"What happened after the truth got out about the test?" I asked.

"Ty was suspended. His father was humiliated, and ... well, he resigned. That's not the worst of it, though. His father committed suicide. When Ty returned to school, he wasn't the same kid he'd been before. He was angry, full of rage over what happened."

"Did Ty confront Jackson about it?"

"He sure did. I was at my locker before first period started, and I heard two guys yelling. I looked over and saw Ty shove Jackson into the lockers. He wrapped a hand around Jackson's neck and started choking him. Took a couple of minutes for teachers to break it up."

"What happened afterward?"

Cora glanced at me and said, "After they pulled Ty off Jackson, Ty spit in Jackson's face, and he said he'd make him pay. He'd make us *all* pay."

21

I woke in the middle of the night, realizing I was no longer in the comfort of my own bed. I was outside, lying on an uncomfortable wooden bench. It was night, but a streetlamp overhead shone so bright it was almost blinding. I held a hand in front of my face, trying to shield myself from its glare, and I pushed myself to a sitting position.

A wool blanket slipped off my body, puddling on the ground in front of me. As the warmth of the blanket left my body, I started shivering. I ran my hands up and down my goose-fleshed arms, but it did little to ward off the crisp chill of the night air. I was dressed in the same nightie I'd worn to bed, a light pink, chiffon floor-length gown. No wonder I was freezing.

I sat a minute in silence, trying to figure out where I was and how I got there. As I looked around, trying to familiarize myself with my surroundings, I noticed the bench I was sitting on was inside a park.

Which park ... I wasn't sure.

It was unfamiliar to me, and I didn't recall ever having been there before.

Several feet away from me was a large circular play area filled with sand. It contained a swing set, a seesaw, and a handful of other things for kids to play on. As I took in the scenery around me, I noticed a flicker of movement behind a tree about twenty feet away from where I was sitting.

I leaned forward, squinting.

When I saw no other signs of movement, I wondered if my eyes had deceived me. Perhaps I was alone, after all. Still ... I needed to be sure.

"Is someone there?" I asked.

No response.

And then another flicker of movement.

I *wasn't* alone.

"Look, I know someone is there, standing behind the tree," I said. "Step out into the light so I can see you."

A young man poked his head out from behind the tree and smiled. He began walking toward me, his hands shoved inside of his pockets. Once he was within a few feet of the bench, he lifted a hand and said, "Hi, I'm sorry I didn't say anything before. I hope you don't think I was trying to frighten you. I wasn't."

"I didn't think you were."

"Good."

"Why were you over there, hiding behind a tree?"

"I was waiting for you to wake up." He gestured toward the bench with his hand. "Is it all right if I sit down?"

I nodded, and he took a seat.

As soon as he sat down, I got a good look at him, and I realized I'd seen him before.

"You're Owen, aren't you?" I asked. "I recognize you from the picture in your, ahh—"

"My obituary in the newspaper?"

I was going to say case file, but he got the idea.

"I suppose I *was* Owen, a long time ago," he said.

I looked him up and down and noticed he was dressed in the same clothes he'd been wearing in the photos taken at the crime scene. The back of his head was misshapen and covered in dried blood—blood that had also stained his shirt, his pants, and even his skin. For all the similarities I'd seen between the crime-scene photos and the young man sitting next to me, there was one obvious difference.

Around his neck, he wore a gold chain.

In the photos in the case file, he wasn't wearing one.

I was sure of it.

"Where did you get the gold chain you're wearing?" I asked.

"Football coach. We all have them. Well, all the star players on the team did."

"Star players, including Aidan and Jackson?"

"Yup."

"Were Aidan and Jackson wearing their chains that night at the cabin too?"

Owen shrugged. "I don't know. Can't remember. Why am I here?"

"I suppose you're here because we're in a dream. *My* dream. I believe this is the park Cora was telling me about earlier tonight. She told me she used to come here with you."

"Yeah, guess you could say this park was our place. We came here a bunch of times. Been a while since I've been back. Been a while since I've visited lots of places. Suppose you could say I'm in limbo. We all are."

"When you say *we*, are you referring to Aidan, Jackson, Brynn, and Aubree?"

"Yup."

"Are they here too?"

Owen looked around. "Don't think so."

"Can you communicate with them? Can you tell them you're here, ask them to join us?"

Owen shook his head. "Doesn't work that way."

"How does it work, then?"

"I don't know, to be honest. Sometimes they're just around. Other times, I don't see them for days, months even."

I leaned down and picked up the blanket, spreading it over my legs. "Are you in limbo because your murders haven't been solved?"

"I don't know. Maybe. Seems we're all stuck in this town. Tried going somewhere else. Doesn't work."

"Where can you go?"

"Here. My house. Places in town. The cabin."

I leaned back, trying to decide what direction to go in next. Given I was in a dream, I wasn't even sure it mattered.

"Do you remember what happened that night at the cabin?" I asked.

Owen laced his hands behind his head. "Sorta. The longer it's been since I died, the more fragmented my memories are from that night. Most of the time I feel like I don't know what's true and what isn't anymore."

"The investigation into your murders has been reopened."

He blinked at me, stunned by what I'd just said. "After all this time ... Why?"

"Because your murders have never been solved, and they need to be. Are you aware Cora's back in town?"

He grinned, remaining quiet for a time before he said, "I saw her today. She's older, but ... the moment I laid eyes on her, I knew it was her."

"You saw her here ... at the park, didn't you?"

"Yeah, right where you're sitting. I would give anything to have been able to talk to her. I tried, even though I knew it wouldn't work."

"I'd like to think she still felt your presence somehow. Her time at the park ... well, I think it changed her. When I met her yesterday, she seemed a lot different than she did tonight."

"How do you know Cora?"

"My name is Georgiana Germaine," I said. "I am a private investigator. Cora has asked me to investigate the murders again. I talked to some of my friends over at the police department about it, and I found out one of the original detectives who worked the case before had asked to reopen it. Looks like we're all working together on this one."

"Guess I don't understand why everyone is so interested after all this time."

"It's been hard on Cora. I don't think she'll ever feel safe until the person who attacked you all is caught. Until then, I think a part of her will always live in fear."

Owen looked away and said, "I miss her."

"She misses you."

"Is she married? Kids?"

"No husband, no kids. Were you aware she had feelings for you?"

"Yeah, I thought as much. She confirmed it today when she was here, talking about what it's been like to go through life without me."

Not knowing how long I had until I woke from the dream, I changed the subject. "I know you said your memories have changed over the years, but I'd like to talk to you about what you still remember about the night you died."

"I'll try. What do you want to know?"

"You were the first one who was attacked. I believe it happened when you went out to your car."

"It did."

"Tell me about the attack."

He leaned forward and bent down, looking at the grass. "I was inside the cabin, and I realized I'd left my glasses in the car. I went out to get them, opened the car door, and leaned in to grab them. Next thing I know, I feel something, a pain in the back of my head. Felt like I'd been hit by a piece of wood or a bat or something."

"What did you do?"

"I backed out of the car and tried turning around so I could see who hit me."

"And did you? Were you able to get a look at the man who assaulted you?"

"Not a good look, no. My mind was kinda fuzzy after that. I remember thinking the guy was taller than me. Bigger too. Before I could get a better look, he hit me again."

"So, you never saw his face?"

Owen shook his head. "It all happened so fast. I didn't have time to shout or to warn the others. There was no time for anything. He whacked me a second time, and I fell to the ground."

"Were you still conscious?"

"Must have been, for a minute, anyway. I remember him grabbing my feet and then dragging me somewhere. I remember the smell of flowers in the air."

"The police found you on the side of the cabin in Millie's flower garden. Did the man say anything to you?"

"He started to, and then he stopped himself. I heard footsteps. It sounded like he was walking away. I kept telling myself to get up, to find a way to get to the cabin before he did. But I couldn't. I just couldn't."

I turned toward Owen, looking him in the eye as I said, "What's the last thing you remember before you died?"

"I knew I was dying, taking the last breaths I'd ever take in this life. I knew I'd never go home, never see my family again, my friends. I felt so alone, the most alone I've ever felt in my life, and then I heard footsteps walking toward me, and someone bending down ... bending down and whispering into my ear."

"Whispering what?"

Owen took a deep breath in and looked over at me.

"He said ... 'It didn't have to be this way.'"

22

I woke the next morning, thinking about the dream. It was the most interactive dream I'd ever had. And it felt different, maybe because it was more direct. There was more communication, less confusion. And yet, much of it was still open to interpretation.

I was leaning up against my headboard, piecing through the dream, when Giovanni walked in with a glass of orange juice and a plate of sourdough toast. He handed me the glass, set the plate down on my nightstand, and slid in next to me.

"You were tossing and turning throughout the night," he said. "How are you feeling this morning?"

"I had an interesting dream."

He raised a brow. "Was it one of *those* dreams—a dream trying to tell you something?"

"Yes."

"Tell me about it."

I grabbed a piece of toast, took a bite, and thought about how to explain what I'd just experienced. "Most dreams like these are hard for me to interpret. I feel like people speak in riddles, or give me bits and pieces, but not enough context to understand what they want me to know."

"How was this one different?"

"I was at a park not far from Cora's house, except it's a park I've never been to before. Owen was there. He was standing behind a tree at first. He said he was waiting for me to wake up. Then he walked over and sat beside me."

"Owen is the kid who used to be Cora's neighbor, the one she fancied, right?"

"Yes."

"What did he say?"

"He knew Cora was alive, and he knew he was dead. He was aware the other four teens at the cabin were dead too. He made a comment about them being stuck here, in limbo. Seems like they're unable to move on."

"Why do you believe he came to you in your dream? Do you think he was trying to give you a message or a clue about his murderer?"

"I'm not sure he was trying to do anything. It seemed like he just wanted to have a conversation with me."

"What did you talk about?"

"I asked him to tell me what happened right before he died. He didn't say much that I didn't already know. He acted like time had taken a toll, blurring his memories from the events of that night."

"Did he say anything useful to you?"

"It wasn't what he said, it was something I observed. In the crime-scene photos, Owen isn't wearing a chain around his neck. None of the young men are. In my dream, he had a gold chain around his neck. I asked him where he got it, and he said it was a gift from their football coach. All the star players had them."

I pointed at a vintage black satchel sitting on a chair on the opposite side of the room.

"Would you mind grabbing that for me?" I asked.

Giovanni stood, retrieved the bag, and brought it over to me. I undid the flap, opened it, and pulled out the case file. Grabbing the photos, I spread them out on the bed. In the crime-scene photos, Aidan, Jackson, and Owen did not have a chain around their necks.

"Maybe it's a clue, and maybe it isn't," I said. "It's worth talking to Whitlock and Harvey, to be sure. I don't remember reading anything in the case file about missing gold chains, but one of the parents could have mentioned it."

My phone buzzed.

I grabbed it off the nightstand and looked at the time, realizing I'd slept in a lot later than I'd planned. I needed to get up and get going. The buzzing sound was a text message from Hunter, asking me if I'd gotten the address she'd sent over for Xander's place. I confirmed I had.

"What is it?" Giovanni asked.

I took a few more bites of toast, drank the orange juice, and tossed the blankets to the side, sliding out of bed.

"Hunter sent me Xander Thornton's address yesterday," I said. "He's the kid who was bullied in school. The good news is, he's not far. He lives in Cayucos."

23

I showered and dressed in one of my favorite vintage skirts—black, knee-length, and pleated—a white, short-sleeved knit cardigan, and red and white, T-strap Mary Janes.

As I headed to the door, Luka circled around me, indicating his desire to be my sidekick for the day. I bent down, giving him a long scratch behind the ears as I said, "Not this time, buddy. Soon, I promise."

He gave me a look that indicated he wasn't pleased, and then he trotted off toward Giovanni. He stopped halfway and turned back as if giving me a chance to change my mind, and I almost did. But I expected today would be a busy one. Being my sidekick would have to wait.

Cayucos was a short twenty-minute drive from Cambria. As I made my way toward Xander's place, I ran through questions I wanted to ask him when I saw him in person.

I wanted to know why he hadn't turned Jackson and the others in after what they did to him.

I wanted to know why he'd prank-called some of the young women he went to school with back then.

And, I wanted to know why he'd cried at the funerals of high school kids who'd treated him as poorly as they had.

Had his tears been an act to make him seem innocent?

Or had his emotions been real?

I mulled those questions over as I turned onto his street.

Xander lived on a quiet cul-de-sac in a sage green house with a wooden exterior and a large back deck overlooking the ocean. The property alone had to have been worth a half-million dollars, I guessed, which suggested Xander had come a long way since high school.

I parked in the driveway behind a black Mercedes-Benz, walked to the front door, pressed the doorbell, and waited. From inside the house, I heard music playing. Blues music by the sounds of it.

A tall, broad-shouldered, brown-haired man answered the door, whistling to the tune of B.B. King's "The Thrill is Gone." He was barefoot and dressed in a black T-shirt and black pants without a belt, which caused his pants to sag around his waist.

The man smiled at me and said, "Can I help you?"

"Are you Xander Thornton?" I asked.

"I sure am. Who might you be?"

"My name's Georgiana Germaine. I'm a private investigator, and I am looking into a series of cold-case murders—murders I'm sure you'll remember."

Xander ran a hand along his chin. "Lemme guess. You're talking about the murders out at Millie Callahan's cabin."

"I am."

"I heard Cora was back in town. Is it true?"

The comment was said in a matter-of-fact manner, like he didn't mind me knowing he was aware of her return. I wondered if he'd come to regret making such a comment after I started questioning him.

"What makes you think Cora has returned home?" I asked.

"A friend of mine told me, one of our old classmates. He saw Cora at the grocery store a couple of days back. Said he didn't recognize her at first, but when he got a bit closer, he was sure it was Cora all right. He tried to strike up a conversation, but she didn't seem to have any interest, and she walked away while he was still talking."

"I wonder why."

"I wonder why myself. She was always a bit skittish. Suppose some things never change. If you're a private investigator, I'm guessing someone hired you to investigate the murders. Mind telling me who?"

I did mind.

I minded a lot.

It was information I wasn't comfortable sharing—not yet.

"There are people in Cambria who still think about what happened that night at the cabin," I said. "People who are uncomfortable knowing the murders were never solved, and the murderer hasn't faced justice."

"People like Cora, for example?"

He'd smirked when he said it, like he already knew she had been the one to hire me.

"I'm not the only one trying to figure out what happened to those teens all those years ago," I said. "The detectives who worked on the case back then have just been given the green light by the chief of police to reopen the investigation too."

Xander crossed his arms and said, "Took them long enough. When the police realized they weren't getting anywhere with the case, they just gave up."

"They *didn't* give up."

"I don't know what else you'd call it. Seems like they gave up to me."

"What matters is we're looking into it again now. And this time, the person responsible for those murders will get what's coming to him."

"What makes you so sure?"

I ignored his query and said, "I'm here because I'd like to ask you a few questions."

He leaned against the doorway, blinking at me but saying nothing. It was possible getting him to play ball might prove to be harder than I thought.

I softened my approach and tried again.

"They're routine questions," I said. "I've been trying to talk to anyone and everyone who knew your classmates around the time the murders occurred."

A moment of silence, and then, "The police suspected me of the murders. They pegged me as one of their main suspects."

"I know."

"Then you understand why I'm leery to speak to anyone."

"I've looked over the file. You had an alibi the night the teens were murdered. Your father said you were with him all night."

"I always thought the police didn't believe him, even though this is supposed to be a country where people are innocent until proven guilty. And yet, sometimes the cops seem sure of a person's guilt long before the case goes to court."

"We all form opinions about each other. It's human nature."

Xander tipped his head to the side, staring at me as he said, "Don't get me wrong. I'm a law-abiding citizen. I believe in the system. I believe in law enforcement too. But I can tell you one thing—when the long arm of the law is pointing a finger at you, it sure doesn't feel good."

"I'm not here to point fingers. I'm here to ask questions."

"Yeah ... well, I'll tell you what I told them. I had nothing to do with the murders. My dad was telling the truth. We were together when the murders took place."

He sounded truthful, but Xander's father was no longer living.

There was no one to dispute his story.

I thought about the way Cora had described Xander to me, but the boy he was then was a lot different than the man he was now.

"If you're innocent, there's no reason not to talk to me about the case, right?"

He shrugged. "I suppose not. You seem like a nice lady."

I was sure there were those who wouldn't agree with his term of endearment, but I had my moments.

"So you'll talk to me, then?" I asked.

Xander swished a hand through the air, swung the front door all the way open, and said, "Come on in."

I followed him down a hallway. Staggered along the walls on both sides were a series of photos in white wooden frames. Several of the photos were of a little girl at various stages in her life. First as a baby, then a toddler, then a child. In the most recent one, she looked to be around twelve years old. In the center of the wall was a photo that was much larger than the rest. In it, Xander was smiling for the camera, standing next to a woman and that same little girl.

Was the woman his wife, and the child *his* child?

I'd know soon enough.

We entered a sitting room, and Xander gestured for me to take a seat on a black leather sofa. He sat across from me in a chair, folding his hands on top of each other as he waited for me to say something.

I started off easy.

"The photo of you in the hallway," I said. "Are the other two in the picture your wife and daughter?"

Xander cleared his throat, his attention switching from me to a large, leaf-shaped tray, filled with fake fruit, resting on the coffee table between us.

"My wife and daughter, yes. My wife ... she ... ahh, she died last year in a car accident. This weekend marks a year since she left us."

I recalled an incident I remembered seeing on the news a year before. A woman had died after a drunk driver ran a red light, plowing right through the front of her car. Was his wife the one who'd died that night?

"I didn't know about your wife," I said. "Did she die after being hit by a drunk driver?"

"Sure did." He bent his head toward the leaf-shaped tray. "My wife had a pottery studio. Made all kinds of things. Sold them at craft festivals. People came from all over America to buy the things she made."

"I'm sorry about what happened to her," I said.

"Yeah, me too. Feel lost without her, you know? She was the glue, the one person who made everything okay in this life. And she was a far better parent than I'll ever be to our daughter, Lila. I'm doing my best, but most of the time, I feel like I'm treading water, like I'm not doing a good enough job. Nothing I'll ever do can compare to how good of a parent my wife was when she was alive."

What he'd just said spoke volumes about him as a person, and I found myself seeing him in a different light. He loved his wife, and he loved his daughter.

But time had a way of changing people.

Had it changed him too?

"The best parents I know feel the same way you're feeling now," I said. "I like to think it makes them better parents. Not because they're perfect, but because they care enough to be better, the best version of themselves for their children."

"I do the best I can."

I crossed a leg over the other and said, "If you don't mind me asking, how is your daughter coping with the loss of her mother?"

Xander blew out a long, heavy breath. "As best as she can. She's quiet, doesn't say a lot."

"Was she always quiet?"

"Lila was a ball of wild energy before my wife passed away."

"Perhaps she needs time to process what happened."

"I get the impression you're speaking from experience."

"My niece lost her father a few years ago. She was seven at the time."

Xander raised a brow. "How's she doing now?"

"Better. Therapy helped her get through it. Do you have any help or support system around?"

"My brother is going through a divorce. I told him he could move in with us. Lila's always been close to him, so having him here has been a positive change in her life."

As he was talking, another man entered the room. He was dressed like Xander in a white T-shirt and black pants, but he was slenderer in build. In his hand he held a sandwich wrapped inside a paper towel. He looked at Xander and said, "Here's the sandwich you asked me to make for—"

The man's attention shifted from Xander to me, and then he said, "Oh, hello."

"Hello," I said.

"This is my brother, Marcus, the one I was telling you about," Xander said.

I introduced myself and explained the reason why I was there.

Marcus nodded and sat in a chair next to his brother, running a hand through his thick, black hair as he said, "I've often wondered if the investigation would ever start up again. Shame it was never solved."

"Giorgiana's confident she'll find the person who's responsible for the murders this time around," Xander said.

"Don't see why not," Marcus said. "You ever seen *Cold Case Files* on TV? Been off the air for a while now, but it's fascinating stuff. With all the advances in forensics, I bet a lot of cold cases could be solved. You been a private eye for a while?"

"I've been in law enforcement for a long time. I used to be a detective for the San Luis Obispo Police Department. I left the position a few years back and opened my own private investigation agency with a couple of friends. They're also former detectives."

"What made you decide to look into the case?" Marcus asked.

"I was hired."

As much as I was enjoying the vigor of our conversation, my objective was to question Xander, *not* to be questioned myself.

"Marcus, are you older or younger than Xander?" I asked.

"I'm one year older."

"You must have been in high school at the same time, then."

"For a year," Xander said. "I was a sophomore when my brother was a senior."

The math wasn't adding up, and then I remembered Cora saying Xander may have been held back a grade or two.

"You were in the eleventh grade when you moved to Cambria, right?" I asked.

"Yes, ma'am," Xander said.

"Where did you live before?"

"Colorado. Our dad got laid off, and my uncle hired him as a salesperson in his furniture shop in town. We've been in the area ever since."

"And your mother?"

Xander cleared his throat and said, "We don't know."

"What do you mean you don't know?"

"She took off with another guy when we were kids. We were raised by our father."

Interesting.

I sat there a moment, thinking about Cora's observation about Xander and mental illness. If he did suffer, he seemed normal now. Nothing in his demeanor suggested he struggled with mental issues—not yet, anyway.

"I'd like to talk about your classmates who died at the cabin," I said.

"What about them?" Xander asked.

"I heard they picked on you at school."

He shrugged and said, "It was high school. Everyone gets picked on or messed with at some point, don't they? Even you, I bet."

Not me.

I was as tough back then as I was now.

And I had brothers—older brothers—who were protective of their sisters.

No one dared to mess with me.

"You don't seem affected by the way you were treated back then, Xander," I said.

"I'm not. It's not worth it to carry ill feelings about past experiences through your life. The only one you end up hurting is yourself."

Wise words.

"He wasn't picked on too much," Marcus said. "Just a bit of harmless teasing among his peers, from what I can remember."

A bit of harmless teasing?

When it came to bullying, we seemed to have differing opinions on what was harmless and what wasn't.

"How is getting your brother drunk, tying him to a tree, and putting a sign around his neck suggesting he's a stalker and a pervert *harmless* teasing?"

Xander's face went red.

I couldn't tell if it was because he was embarrassed, or because his anger had flared up, or both.

Marcus stared at me, his expression one of confusion.

"I'm not sure what you're talking about," Marcus said. "You must be mistaken. My brother was never tied to a tree in a park. If he was, I would have known about it."

I looked at Xander and said, "Is there anything you want to say?"

"There's nothing *to* say," Marcus said, "except ... you've got the wrong guy."

24

The three of us sat in silence for a time, and I waited for Xander to tell his brother what happened to him when he was in high school. But Xander didn't seem interested in talking or in clearing up the confusion. He stared at the floor, somber and grim, like he wanted the conversation to end, but I saw no way forward until we tackled the demons from his past.

Marcus made a few more attempts to get Xander to talk. When his efforts didn't yield a result, he shifted the conversation back my way.

"Who told you my brother was tied to a tree when he was in high school?" Marcus asked.

"Who told me doesn't matter," I said. "What matters is that the story is true. Your brother was bullied by several of his fellow classmates."

"Who would have done such a thing? And why? What did my brother do to warrant that kind of treatment?"

"The ringleader and his friends were the same teens who were murdered," I said. "They picked on your brother at school sometimes. They teased him, berated him, pretended like they wanted to be his friend, even though they didn't. They lured him to the park, got him drunk, stripped him down to his underwear, and then hung a sign around his neck."

Marcus looked at Xander. "Is what she's saying true? Tell me."

Without looking up, Xander nodded and said, "Let's not do this right now, okay?"

"Uhh ... we're doing it," Marcus said. "I want to know what happened that day in the park."

"Why? It's in the past. It doesn't matter now."

"It *does* matter," Marcus said. "I don't understand why you never told me."

The fact Marcus knew nothing about the extent to which his brother had been treated in high school came as a surprise.

What else didn't he know?

Marcus shook his head, leaning back in the chair as he huffed out an irritated, "Come on, Xander. Talk to me. I need to know why this is the first time I'm hearing this story."

Xander looked up, and I leaned toward him, curious to know what he was about to say.

"Dad thought it was best not to talk about it, so we didn't," Xander said. "You remember how Dad was about this stuff. He didn't like drama, didn't like to admit that I wasn't liked or accepted in school. He wanted us both to be tough. To complain about anything, no matter how big or small, was seen as a sign of weakness. To show emotion of any kind was ... well, unacceptable."

"Dad was an avoider, yes," Marcus said. "He hated talking about feelings, about anything that mattered. I'm not him. You could have come to me. I would have listened. I would have been there for you."

"You'd moved to Visalia, and you were busy with your own life. Besides, it wasn't like I wanted to admit what they did to me. I wasn't proud of it."

"Why *did* they treat you that way?"

Xander glanced in my direction, studying my face like he was trying to decide if I knew the entire story or just bits and pieces of it.

Did I know about the prank calls the girls thought he'd made, the heavy breathing, the word game he'd played with Aubree? Rather than keep him in suspense, I decided to shed light on what I'd been told.

"I know about the phone calls you made, Xander," I said.

"What phone calls?" Marcus asked.

Xander buried his head in his hands.

For such a strong, brawny man, he appeared fragile and weak to me now, much more like the boy Cora had described.

Frustrated, Marcus pressed his brother for information, saying, "What phone calls?"

Xander lowered his voice. "I don't know what to say."

"Say something," Marcus said, arms splayed. "Because right now, I don't understand any of it."

"I'm not in the right frame of mind to have this conversation," Xander said. "I'm going through a lot right now. I don't want to drag my past into it, all right? I can't. I just ... I can't."

Marcus faced me and said, "*You* can. Can't you?"

I supposed most people in my current predicament would have felt awkward to be put into a position like the one Marcus had just put me in. But since Xander remained quiet and hadn't piped up with an objection about me filling in the gaps, I decided to accommodate his brother's request.

"In Xander's senior year of high school, some of his female classmates started receiving prank phone calls," I said. "The male who made the calls waited for the girls to answer, and then he breathed heavily into the phone while saying the girls' names."

"That's it? No threats or anything?"

"Not as far as I know."

"Why do you assume my brother is to blame?"

"During one of the calls, he played a word game with the young woman on the other end of the line. She believed the caller gave her a scrambled version of his name, which turned out to be Xander."

"Did Xander ever *admit* to making the calls?"

"No," I said. "Not to my knowledge."

"Unless he comes right out and says he did it, I'd bet he didn't. Seems to me the word game was just another way for the school bullies to blame one more thing on my brother."

"Given we're sitting here with your brother, it seems like an easy thing to clear up, wouldn't you say?"

We turned our attention to Xander, and I said, "If you made those calls, now's the time to set the record straight."

Xander remained quiet.

I figured he wasn't going to speak on the matter, but then he looked up, his tear-filled eyes full of remorse, and said, "I never meant to hurt anyone."

"You never meant to hurt anyone," Marcus repeated. "What are you saying?"

"I'm saying ... it was me. I did it. *I* made those calls."

Marcus shot out of his chair, pacing the room as he chastised his brother. "Why in the world would you do such a thing?"

"I ... I don't know. I was bored, and I liked hearing the sound of their voices. I liked knowing they were giving their attention to me."

"They weren't giving their attention to you," Marcus said. "Not willingly. They were scared."

Xander shrugged. "I made a mistake."

Marcus shook his head, looking over at me and saying, "I'm sorry. I think it's best if you go now. I need to speak to my brother in private."

I respected Marcus's position, but I had more questions—questions it seemed I wasn't getting answered today.

Marcus walked me out of the room, his expression one of dismay and confusion.

He opened the front door and said, "This doesn't change anything. My brother may have made some inappropriate phone calls because he was seeking attention. It doesn't make him a killer."

I walked to the car wondering who Marcus was trying to convince about Xander's innocence more—me ... or himself?

25

Simone and Hunter were sitting on the sofa, laughing, when I walked into the office.

I sat beside them, brow raised. "What's so funny?"

"Simone just told me a joke," Hunter said. "Want to hear it?"

"Sure."

"What name would a detective use if she decided to open a real estate business?"

I gave the question some thought.

Nothing came to mind at first.

And then ...

"I'm guessing it has something to do with a play on the word *homes*," I said. "You know, as in Sherlock Holmes."

Hunter shook her head and said, "Shoot, you're no fun."

"Why? Because I guessed it right?"

"Close enough—the real estate business would be called Holmes Homes."

Corny, but cute.

I moved the conversation in a more serious direction.

"Simone, have you spoken to the victims' families?" I asked.

"I was just going to message you about what I've found out," Simone said. "Brynn and Aubree's parents no longer live in the area. Brynn's parents are in Texas, and Aubree's moved to North Carolina."

"Did you talk to them?"

"I spoke to Brynn's mother on the phone. She made it clear they've left their daughter's murder in the past. They want no involvement in our investigation. She asked me not to call again, and then she hung up on me."

I understood Brynn's mother's reaction to Simone's call.

Dredging up the painful past would prove too hard for some to bear, a pain they wouldn't want to go through a second time.

"What about Aubree's parents?" I asked. "Did you speak to them?"

"They divorced about a year after Aubree was murdered. I left a couple of messages for her mother. She hasn't returned my calls. Her father talked to me, but he said nothing of significance. He doesn't believe he could be of any help with our investigation."

Tough crowd.

But not unexpected.

"Seems like you struck out with the girls' parents," I said. "What about Aidan, Jackson, and Owen? Do their families still live in the area?"

"Not in Cambria, but close enough. They're all in the central coast. I've met with all three of the boys' parents. Which family visit do you want to hear about first?"

Based on what I knew about them so far, Jackson had seemed to be the orchestrator when it came to stirring up trouble. He also had a controlling stepfather whose negative influence could have been the reason for Jackson's rebellious behavior.

I started out easy.

"Tell me about Owen," I said. "Everything I know about him leads me to believe he was a good person, someone who could be relied upon. I'll bet he was a good support system to his friends, and in some cases, he acted as the voice of reason."

"Everything you've heard is in line with what his parents told me," Simone said. "I wasn't at their house five minutes before they whipped out his baby books. And when I say baby books, they have a book for each year of his life."

"How do they feel about us looking into the murders again?"

"Both parents are on board. His mother started crying when I mentioned it, and his father said he hopes we catch the guy this time. Both parents are willing to assist us in any way they can."

"Sounds like they're good people."

"Two of the nicest people I've ever met. Super religious, too."

"In what way?"

"Owen's mother prays for the man who murdered their son. Even though she doesn't know who he is, she told me she's forgiven him in her heart. She believes it was the only way she could accept what happened and move on."

Simone raised a brow, exchanging a curious glance with Hunter.

"What is it?" I asked.

"It's nothing," Simone said.

"It's something."

"It's just ... you're doing the thing."

"What *thing*?"

"The thing you do ... you know, with your fingers."

Simone pointed at my hands, and I looked down.

"You rub your fingers for two reasons. One, when you're nervous. And two, when there's something you're keeping from everyone else. And you don't get nervous often. So ... is there anything you'd like to tell us?"

She was far more observant than I realized.

"I'm not keeping anything from the two of you," I said. "What I mean to say is ... yes, there's something I haven't mentioned, but it's not because I'm trying to keep it to myself. It just happened last night."

Simone and Hunter leaned in, smiling.

"Do tell," Hunter said.

"Yes," Simone added. "Please do."

"I had a dream last night," I said. "And before you ask ... yes, it was *that* kind of dream."

"Ooh, tell us about it," Simone said. "Give us all the juicy details."

"I was in the park. Owen was there. He said something about not being able to move on from this life to the next." I filled them in on the rest of the dream, ending with, "What's important is, Owen looked just like he did in the crime-scene photos. He had on the same clothing he was wearing when he died. His wounds were the same. But there was one key difference. In my dream, he was wearing a chain around his neck. In the photos in the case file, he isn't wearing one."

"Do you think it holds some significance?" Simone asked.

"It might."

"What did the chain look like?"

"It was gold and thick. Some of the boys on the football team received them from their coach."

"Huh," Simone said. "Give me a second."

She reached into one of her pant pockets, pulled out her cell phone, and clicked on her photos. She began flipping through them, saying, "Nope. Nope. Not in this one either."

A few more swipes, and she smiled, turning the phone around as she pointed at a photo of Owen, Aidan, and Jackson. They were all standing next to each other, arm in arm.

"Chains like these?" Simone asked.

I bent down, narrowing my eyes as I took a good look.

"Yes," I said. "Where did you get this photo?"

"Owen's mother gave me a tour of his bedroom while I was there. They haven't touched a single thing in it since he died. I snapped a bunch of photos he had pinned to a corkboard above his dresser. This was one of them."

Hunter piped up, saying, "Do you think they were wearing the chains the day they died?"

"I think it's possible," I said.

"His mother said they wore them all the time," Simone said.

"Given they weren't in the crime-scene photos, it makes me wonder whether they had them on that day. If so, it would mean someone removed them from around their necks."

"The girls wouldn't have been wearing matching jewelry, I'd guess," Simone said. "Why take something from the boys and not the girls?"

"Maybe the killer took something from them as well."

"If he did, it's not in the case file, and as far as I know, none of the parents mentioned anything about missing items."

"Serial killers are known for keeping items from their victims as trophies," Hunter said. "But we're dealing with a mass murderer in my opinion, not a serial killer. Serial killers almost always strike again, and this guy hasn't, as far as we know."

I gave Hunter's comments some thought.

"I'm not sure why none of the parents mentioned a missing chain their sons may have been wearing the day they died," I said. "And we don't know for sure whether any items were taken from the girls or not. Maybe a memento *was* taken. As to your comment about an item being removed as a trophy, I suppose it's possible. But the more I think about it, the more I believe there would have been another reason for doing what he did."

"A reason like ...?"

"If we consider what we know, they were all murdered in a brutal way. It's like whoever killed the teens that day was angry. I'd even go so far as to say he felt hatred toward them and even justified in what he did. Removing the chains could have been because he felt they were unworthy of them."

It was just a guess, mere speculation.

We didn't know if the chains were even worn by the boys that day.

"So what now?" Simone asked.

Now we get back to the topic at hand.

"Let's set our theories to the side for a moment and discuss your visit with Aidan's parents, Simone."

Simone rolled her eyes.

"That bad, eh?" I said.

"Aidan's parents are a piece of work," she said.

"In what way?"

"In every way. Rich, hoity-toity types. They have six children, and to hear them talk about Aidan ... it was almost like it wasn't a big deal to lose one kid when five of their other kids are still alive. I don't mean to suggest they didn't love him. I'm saying they live their lives for the children they have left. The way they talk about Aidan is almost like he never existed, like he's nothing more than a fleeting memory."

"How could a parent do such a thing?" Hunter asked.

I could think of a reason why.

It made the loss of their son more bearable. For some people, pretending a loved one never existed was a lot easier than living with the pain that came with knowing they had no choice but to live the rest of their lives without their beloved.

"What did Aidan's parents say about him?" I asked.

"Not much. They visit his grave once a year on his birthday. Oh, and at Thanksgiving dinner, they go around the table and honor his life with a memory, something they remember about him. Other than those two days, they prefer not to discuss him at all."

Pretending they were fine didn't mean they were. Without processing their son's death, they never would heal—not to the fullest extent.

"What do they think about the case being investigated again?" I asked.

"They were ambivalent and didn't seem to care either way. They wished us luck on solving the case, but they believe the killer wasn't caught then and he won't be caught now."

And then there was one.

"We've got your visits with Aidan and Owen's parents out of the way," I said. "Let's talk about Jackson."

"Ahh, Jackson," Simone said. "My visit with his mother and stepfather was interesting, if not surprising. I'll start by saying this ... you saved the best for last."

26

"I learned a few more interesting details about Jackson last night when I spoke to Cora," I said. "It sounds like he had a troubled home life."

"We know about how he treated Xander," Hunter said. "Is there something else?"

"He cheated on his final biology exam."

Hunter snickered a laugh. "A lot of kids cheat on exams."

"The circumstances surrounding this instance are a bit more complicated. Jackson cheated because if he didn't pass the exam with a good enough grade, his stepfather threatened to withhold the college money his mother had set aside for him."

I shared the story Cora had told me, including the fallout afterward.

"If Jackson's mother set aside money for his education, it should have been up to her whether or not Jackson was given the money," Hunter said. "Why did the stepdad get involved?"

"Trust me," Simone said. "You'd know if you met him. The stepdad's a real piece of work."

"Tell us about your visit with him," I said.

Simone raised a finger. "I will, but first, I need coffee. Anyone else?"

"I ... ahh, I need to get going," Hunter said. "My sister's in town. We're meeting for lunch. I'll be back later. In the meantime, text me if you need me to do anything for you, Georgiana, okay?"

"There is one thing. Look into Jackson's stepdad. See what you can find out about him."

"Will do."

Simone headed to the kitchen to try out the fancy Breville coffeemaker I'd just purchased for the office. She had a habit of stopping for coffee on her way into the office each morning, which almost always made her late on the days when I scheduled a meeting between us. In a way, buying a machine for the office was serving my own agenda, but it also came with its perks.

Simone and I reconvened on the sectional sofa a few minutes later, fresh-brewed coffees in hand.

"Jackson's stepfather, Ray, had nothing nice to say about him," Simone said. "The way he talked about Jackson was almost like he was glad Jackson was dead."

"And his mother?" I asked. "What did she have to say?"

"Her name is Valerie. She was quiet, didn't say much of anything the entire time I was there. Ray did most of the talking."

"Tell me about your conversation."

Simone took a sip of her coffee and set her mug down on a coaster on the side table. "It wasn't a long visit, so I may as well start at the beginning and take you through it. Ray answered the door before I even had a chance to knock."

"What's he like?"

"Sharp dresser. He was wearing a gray tailored suit. It looked expensive."

"How would you describe his physical appearance?"

"He's muscular. Looks like he works out a fair bit."

"How tall is he?"

"Just over six feet, I'd guess."

"What does he do for work?" I asked. "Is he still working in the family business?"

"He is, and this is where it gets interesting. He's the COO of their high-end car dealership. The dealership was opened by Valerie's father, who had planned on leaving it to Jackson after he retired. When Jackson died, the business was left to Valerie ... though, based on Ray's overbearing personality, I get the impression he's the one running the show."

I didn't even need to meet the guy to know his type—possessive, greedy, arrogant, entitled.

"After Ray greeted you at the door, what happened?" I asked.

"I gave him my name, told him what I do, and I explained I was there because we're taking another look at the case."

"How did Ray react to the news that it's being investigated again?" I asked.

"He seemed confused at first. It took him a minute to grasp what I'd said. I let him know I had a few questions, and I assured him they were nothing major. For a minute, I thought he was going to refuse to speak to me, so I mentioned we were talking to all the families. I thought adding that little tidbit would compel him to be more of a team player."

"Did it work? Did he agree to talk to you?"

"Under certain conditions. Before I was allowed to step foot inside the house, Ray said he didn't want me to say anything that might upset his wife, which is ... as you know, an impossible request. I was there to talk about the murders. No matter how you spin it, it's a heavy subject."

"I'm sure you found a way."

Simone shot me a wink. "We say what we need to say and do what we need to get through the door, right?"

"Right."

"I'm assuming you talked your way inside," I said. "Then what?"

"Ray made a comment about not wanting us to talk inside the house because it was a bit of a mess, which was weird because what I saw of it was immaculate. Everything in its place."

Some people didn't like the idea of a stranger in their home, among their personal things, in their personal space. Other people didn't welcome visitors inside because there was something they were trying to hide.

Which one was Ray?

Neither, or a bit of both?

"I followed him to the back yard, and he told me to take a seat at a patio table," Simone said. "He left me for a few minutes and returned with Valerie. She was wearing a large pair of sunglasses, which made sense. It was sunny out yesterday. But she was dressed in a pair of sweatpants and an oversized sweater. I was sweating in the thin T-shirt I had on."

"Did she acknowledge you in any way?"

"She said hello. It was so faint, I almost didn't hear it. After she sat down, she kept tugging at the collar of her sweater, pulling it up like she was trying to cover her neck." Simone crossed her arms and added, "How do I put this ... she reminded me of a frightened little mouse. She seemed nervous and avoidant."

A woman trapped like a prisoner in her own home, perhaps.

In the time Simone described the beginning of her visit, several things she'd said stood out to me:

Ray didn't want Simone inside the house.

Why?

Valerie was going out of her way to cover herself up.

Why?

I thought about the bruises Aubree told Cora she'd seen on Jackson's shoulder and back.

Had he been abused by Ray?

If so, had Valerie also suffered from abuse, and was she being abused now?

My mind was teeming with various possibilities.

Perhaps Ray hadn't wanted Simone in the house because he worried she'd see signs of his violent behavior. I imagined photos strategically placed on the wall, photos that covered up the places where Ray had used his fist to take out his aggression.

My mind wandered even further.

Was Valerie wearing sunglasses because it was sunny out? Or were the sunglasses in place to conceal a shiner, and the clothes covering almost every inch of her body to hide bruises, signs she was a battered woman.

"Georgiana, are you listening to me?" Simone asked.

Hearing my name snapped me back into reality.

"Sorry, I got a bit fixated on your description of Valerie," I said. "Keep going. I won't lose focus again."

"I was saying we talked about basic stuff at first. I figured it would be easier to talk about the heavier stuff if I tried to get to know them and what their life has been like over the last twenty years. That's how I learned about the car dealership and Ray's role in the company. In his words, he said the last twenty years have been the best of his life."

"Did you believe him?"

"I believe they may have been the best years of *his* life, but I doubt it's been the same for her. Jackson was an only child. He was two years old when his parents divorced. Ray and Valerie met about ten years later, and they've been together ever since."

That would make Jackson twelve years old when Ray entered their lives, and no doubt changed the course of it forever.

"Once you got the initial conversation out of the way, were you able to talk about the investigation?" I asked.

Simone reached for her coffee. "For a few minutes. I asked if they had an opinion about the person responsible for the cabin murders."

"And what did they say?"

"Ray wasted no time throwing Xander's name out, saying he always thought he was to blame. He said the whole town knew Xander was a suspect. There were rumors swirling around town about Xander and how he'd been teased at school by some of the boys on the football team."

"I wonder if they knew about Xander being tied to the tree?"

"If they did, they didn't mention it. They knew about the prank calls some of the girls in school had been receiving."

It was possible what had happened to Xander in the park wasn't public knowledge. He'd downplayed it after it happened, making me wonder if the police had also decided to keep it quiet. It made sense. Had everyone in town known about the incident, I had no doubt they would have pushed for Xander to be blamed for the murders whether he had an alibi or not.

"Is there anything else I should know about your visit?" I asked.

Simone gave the question some thought. "I asked if there were any details they may have forgotten to mention during the initial investigation. Ray said no."

"You said Ray did *most* of the talking. Did Valerie say anything?"

"I was just about to tell you ... toward the end of the conversation, Valerie asked Ray to get her a glass of water. He was reluctant. I could tell he didn't want to leave her side, but he did. As soon as he was out of sight, I slipped her our business card and told her to call us any time, for any reason. She thanked me."

"Did she say anything else?"

"She said she loved her son, and that she missed him. She started to say something else, but before she could get the words out, Ray was back with her glass of water. Got himself one too. Nothing for me, though. Jerk."

"He didn't offer you anything because it would have given you a reason to stay longer. Going off of what you said about him, I bet he wanted you out of there."

"I thought the same thing. As soon as he handed her the water, he said they had some errands to run. I was in and out in less than twenty minutes."

Simone's short visit deserved a followup, one I planned on doing myself. Even if it didn't further the case, I was concerned about Valerie's odd behavior. I wanted to get her alone and see what she might say when Ray wasn't around.

"I'd like their address," I said.

"Why? You thinking about stopping by?"

"It crossed my mind."

Simone reached for her phone, pressed a few buttons, and said, "I just sent it to you. Oh, and there's one more thing I want to add. After I left their house, I started thinking about Valerie's father. I wondered if he was still alive."

"Is he?"

Simone nodded and said, "I had Hunter do a search for him. It was easy because it turns out the house Ray and Valerie are living in is owned by him. His name is Hugo, and he lives in a retirement community in San Luis Obispo. He was sharp as a whip when I spoke to him."

"What did you talk about?"

"I told him I'd just been to see Ray and Valerie to talk to them about the investigation. He told me he doesn't have much contact with his daughter."

"Did he say why?"

"Hugo didn't give me much in the way of details, except to say the fallout between him and Valerie was Ray's doing. He mentioned something about Ray driving a wedge between them. He said he missed his daughter, and he worried the car dealership wasn't being run by her like they had discussed when she took it over. He said if he was younger, he wouldn't allow it, but he feels he's too old and too tired to deal with the stress of it now."

With Jackson dead, and Hugo pushed to the side, Ray had swooped in, taking over the company and lining his pockets along the way. Greed was a good motive for murder, but was it enough of a motive for a mass murder?

On the one hand, it didn't seem realistic.

On the other, there were certain types of people who would do anything to get ahead—including getting rid of anyone who stood in their way to get there.

27

Ty Conroy had followed in his father's footsteps, becoming a biology teacher at the local high school, the same school his father had taught at twenty years earlier. I arrived just as classes had ended for the day, and I found Ty in his classroom, tidying up his desk.

Ty was a tall man and heavyset, with a receding hairline he was struggling to hold on to even though he'd already lost the fight. His shirt, an ill-fitted, short-sleeved button-up, had once been white but now it had a gray tinge to it like it had been washed with a load of darks too many times. And while it appeared he'd tried tucking it into his black trousers at some point earlier in the day, it had come halfway untucked, with baggy areas flapping over the top of his pants.

He didn't see me when I first walked in, but I saw him, reaching into the top of his desk drawer and pulling out a silver flask. He twisted off the cap, bent his head back, and took a long, hearty swig, wiping his mouth afterward as he breathed out the stress of a long school day.

He slid the flask back into the drawer, closed it, and turned, startled to see me standing there, eyeing him with curiosity.

I flashed him a big grin and said, "I feel like this is where I'm supposed to say it's five o'clock somewhere. I mean, not here ... but somewhere."

Here it was three o'clock, not that it mattered.

School was out.

His students were gone.

Who was I to judge the man for taking a wee gulp of liquor if he needed one? I had no idea what kind of day he'd had, or week, or year, for that matter.

"I'm ... uhh, sorry," he said. "I didn't see you come in."

I swished a hand through the air. "It's all right. Take another swig if you need one. Sip, sip away."

I almost laughed after I said it, but he hadn't so much as cracked a smile. He hadn't found my quip as funny as I did, it seemed.

Ty moved a hand to his hip and asked, "Do I know you?"

"I don't think so."

"What are you doing here? Is there something I can do for you?"

"I'm Georgiana Germaine, and I'm a—"

"I'll stop you there. You're investigating the murders of my old classmates. I've heard. Everyone in town has, I expect. Word gets out fast around here."

So it would seem.

"If you know who I am, I'm guessing you also know why I'm here," I said.

"I do not."

Except he did—I could tell.

"Sure you do," I said.

He stared at me for a moment and then said, "I haven't talked to anyone about what happened back then in a long time. I don't know how I can be of any help."

I did.

"I heard an interesting story about you yesterday," I said.

"Oh, yeah?"

"Back when your father taught here, he created a final test for his students, a test he never changed over the years."

"What about it?"

"You knew about the test, knew your father always gave the same one year after year. You slipped a copy to Jackson, so he'd get a good grade. Except it backfired when your father figured out Jackson and a few of his friends had seen it beforehand."

Ty cleared his throat once, then again.

He pointed at the door to the classroom and said, "Would you mind closing it, please? This isn't a conversation I wish to have while faculty members are walking around in the hallway."

I did as he asked, and then I joined him at his desk.

"I haven't thought about what happened back then in ... well, many years," he said. "It's not a memory a person wants to revisit."

"Your father didn't take it well when he found out some of his students had cheated."

"He did not, and he blamed me for all of it. He stopped speaking to me."

Before I'd driven over to the school, I'd taken a moment to read the notes in the case file about the interview Whitlock and Harvey had conducted at Ty's home during the murder investigation, and I learned a few things I didn't know.

"Your father died a week before you graduated from high school," I said. "He overdosed on pain killers."

"Yeah, he did."

"Must have been hard on you, given the two of you weren't speaking."

"My father was recovering from a motor bike accident. He was in a lot of pain, and he was depressed. We didn't realize how bad things were until after he died. I don't ... ahh ... I don't want to talk about him."

"I imagine everything that happened back then was upsetting," I said. "You trusted Jackson with the test. You asked him not to show it to anyone, and he broke your trust. If he hadn't shown it to anyone else, there's a good chance no one would have ever known what happened."

"Why does any of this matter now? Why waste your time coming here to talk to me about it?"

My reasons were forthcoming.

I just had a few more things to say before I gave him the hard press.

"When your father realized some of his students had cheated, he went to the school principal," I said.

"What about it?"

"He was so upset, he retired," I said.

"Who told you that?"

"One of your classmates."

"It isn't true. My father didn't retire because some knuckleheads cheated on a test. He was going to retire anyway. He just hadn't told anyone yet. My mother and I knew, but my dad was waiting to make it official until after school got out for the summer."

Ty seemed nervous, and I wasn't close to being done yet.

He ran a hand along his sweaty brow.

"You assaulted Jackson after the truth came out," I said. "You pushed him up against the lockers and tried to choke him."

"Oh, for goodness' sake ... I don't have time for this right now. This entire conversation, it's ridiculous. What happened with Jackson at his locker wasn't a big deal. I was angry."

"Did you think he wouldn't turn you in if he got caught?" I asked.

"I dunno. Hard to say. He was put in a difficult predicament."

A difficult predicament?

He was playing it off like it meant nothing.

Then again, a lot of time had passed since it happened.

Maybe it wasn't a big deal anymore.

"The day after the test, Jackson and a few of his friends were called into the principal's office," I said. "They didn't admit to cheating, but Jackson's stepdad said he'd seen the test in Jackson's room. The following day, the principal found a note on the door of his office stating you were the one who'd given Jackson the test. I assume you thought Jackson wrote the note because you confronted him. You spit in his face."

"It's not what you think."

"There were eyewitnesses who saw what happened."

"I didn't spit on Jackson on purpose. I was mad, and while I was yelling at him, I got carried away. I wasn't trying to choke him either. I was trying to keep him from taking off until I told him how I felt about what he did."

"I bet I know how you felt when you gave him the test," I said. "You felt accepted. You thought the two of you were friends. You thought you were doing him a solid, a favor no one else could have done except for you."

"I felt bad for the guy. So what?"

"You felt bad for him *before* you gave him the test ... not after everything came out. Someone wrote the note. Someone stuck it on the principal's door, and you decided Jackson did it."

Ty opened his desk drawer. I thought he was going to reach for the flask again, but he didn't. He grabbed a bottle of water, opened it, and drank it halfway down. Then he slammed it down on the desk, shaking his head as he said, "I confronted Jackson that day, yes. I asked if he'd written the note. He started laughing, and he just kept on laughing while everyone looked on."

"You threatened him. You said you'd make him pay. You said you'd make them *all* pay."

"I was heated. It was a stupid thing to say. I should have never said it. For all I know, any one of them could have written that note."

I tapped a fingernail on the top of his desk, thinking about what he'd just said to me. "I'm trying to figure out why you're defending Jackson, even now, a kid who I've heard was a school bully at times.

Why not be honest about how you feel? What does it matter now?"

Ty downed the rest of the water and said, "He's *dead*! Why would I speak ill of him now? I'm alive. *I'm* still living. He died too young. They all did, lost their lives to some violent maniac who's still free because the cops in this town couldn't do their job!"

There it was, the anger I'd been pushing for, needling him bit by bit until I wore him down. His anger showed me he still had a temper after all these years. And even though twenty years had passed, not only did he still blame Jackson, but I believed he hadn't forgiven Jackson for his betrayal.

"When the police interviewed your family, your mother said you were with her the night Jackson and the others died," I said. "I read it in the police file. Is that true?"

"I was at home all night, just like she said."

"Funny thing about parents ... many will do anything to protect their child whether they're guilty or innocent."

"Is that why you're here—to accuse me of murdering five people?"

And attempted murder of a sixth.

"I haven't accused you of anything." I pointed at the sleeve of his shirt. "You've got what looks like a reddish stain on your shirt sleeve, at the bottom, by the cuff."

Ty raised his wrist, staring at what I'd just pointed out. "I don't know what that is or how it got there."

I steered the conversation in a more pointed direction.

"Must have been hard for Cora, to be the only one to survive the attack," I said. "She's lucky to be alive ... gone but not forgotten."

Gone but not forgotten, the words left on the cabin wall.

I wondered how he'd react when he heard them.

But he had no reaction, none at all.

"I was relieved when I heard Cora survived," he said. "She was a nice person, from what I remember about her, at least."

"I took a trip up to the cabin yesterday where it all happened.

There was a message written on one of the bedroom walls. And sure, I suppose it could be old. But I think it's new. I think the killer is still around. He's sent a message to Cora to incite fear, to make sure she knows he knows she's still alive."

"Huh, I'm surprised. I heard the family hasn't been to the cabin for years. Students go up there on a dare from time to time. They're convinced the cabin is haunted. You know how stories like that go. Everyone's always curious about a murder house."

"I suppose they are."

"You want to know what's crazy about it all? Detectives came to my house back then because they considered me a suspect. *Me*, someone who's never been in an altercation in his life."

"But you have been in an altercation ... with Jackson."

Ty rolled his eyes. "That doesn't count."

"Doesn't it?" I asked.

"He didn't get hurt." Ty leaned over his desk, grabbed a stack of papers, and stuffed them into a worn, brown-leather satchel dangling off the side of his desk chair. "If there's nothing else ... I need to get going."

"I suppose I've troubled you enough for now."

"For now? What? You think I'm a suspect too?"

"Maybe. Whether you are or you aren't, I'll know soon enough."

Ty slung the satchel over his shoulder, flashing me a snarky grin as he said, "You think you're smart? You think I'm your guy? Prove it."

I smiled back. "Oh, don't worry. If you're guilty, I will."

28

I was at my mother's house, sitting on the back deck with Harvey and Whitlock, talking about my day.

"During your investigation, did any of the boys' parents mention a gold chain their son had been given from their football coach?" I asked.

Harvey shrugged. "Shoot, I can't remember. Was a gold chain mentioned in the case file?"

"No," I said.

"Then why are you asking about it?"

"When I was at the office earlier, I was talking to Simone, and she said—"

Harvey's eyes lit up, and he held up a hand. "Sorry to interrupt. Now that I'm thinking about it, I seem to remember Owen's mother mentioning a chain her son always wore. She thought he may have been wearing it the day he died, but she wasn't sure. A small detail, of course. Still, I was sure I mentioned it somewhere in my notes."

Except he hadn't.

The sliding glass door slid open, and my mother stuck her head out, eyeing the three of us with curiosity. "You three had better not be talking about the investigation without me. You aren't, are you?"

I wasn't about to admit what we'd been discussing, so I kept quiet.

Whitlock, on the other hand, piped up with, "We've been waiting for Georgiana to tell us about her day. I thought we could all discuss it over dinner. The aroma coming from the kitchen is divine, I might add. Whatever feast you've prepared for us, I'm sure it will be wonderful."

His clever, complimentary response skirted the issue at hand, flattering her in a way that seemed to satisfy her concerns.

"I've cooked a pot roast," my mother said. "And I cooked up some roast potatoes, just the way you like them, Georgiana."

"I appreciate it, Mom," I said.

"And I'd appreciate seeing my daughter's beautiful face more often." She shot me a wink and added, "Dinner will be ready in ten minutes."

She pulled the sliding glass door closed, humming, as she disappeared inside the house.

Whitlock crossed one leg over the other, offering a peek at the colorful bright blue socks he was wearing. He leaned closer to me and whispered, "All right, there's no way you'd mention a gold chain without a good reason, so let's hear it."

"As I'd started to say before, I caught up with Simone earlier about her visits with the teens' parents," I said.

"Who has she talked to so far?"

"She's visited with Owen and Jackson's parents. Owen's mother offered to show her his bedroom. It's remained untouched since his death. There was a corkboard on the wall with photos. In one of them, the boys were standing next to each other, wearing the gold chains they'd been given by their coach."

Harvey leaned back in his chair, staring through the kitchen window.

He looked nervous.

"Do you think we should wait to talk about this at dinner?" Harvey asked. "Happy wife, happy life, and all that."

Whitlock elbowed Harvey. "Oh, don't be such a ninny. I'm sure Georgiana has plenty more to say about her day, which we'll discuss over dinner. Let's finish the topic at hand and save the rest for the dinner table. Deal?"

Although hesitant, Harvey nodded, saying, "Keep going, Gigi. What are you thinking?"

"If the boys wore the gold chains all the time, it's reasonable to assume they had them around their necks the night they died. And yet, they aren't in any of the crime scene photos."

"Maybe the killer took them as a memento," Whitlock said. "A token of his crime to help him relive that night."

I wasn't so sure.

"I think we're dealing with a different type of killer," I said. "The man hasn't murdered again in two decades."

"That we know of," Harvey said. "He could have moved, picked up where he left off in a new location."

"I have a theory about the gold chains," I said. "If he took them, I believe it was to prove a point. The chains gave the boys status. They were only given to the star football players. Strip them of the chains, you strip them of their status, making them appear no different than anyone else."

My mother knocked on the glass door, waving us inside. As we stood up, I turned to Harvey and said, "Hey, have you had a chance to talk to her about how you've been feeling?"

"I ... ahh ... I, well—"

"So no, then."

"I decided to make it as easy as possible on both of us. I told her I didn't want the investigation to cause me too much stress, so I've decided to let you and Whitlock do your thing. She knows you'll check in by way of text message or maybe even a call here and there so I can stay up on things."

"I bet she's thrilled," I said.

"Sure is ... why else do you think she's humming? Been humming to herself all day."

We joined my mother at the table.

As we filled our plates with comfort food, she said, "How was your day, Georgiana? Have any suspects yet?"

"A few. How was your day?"

Harvey looked at my mother and then said, "We had a bit of a scare this morning."

"What do you mean?"

"It's nothing to fuss over," my mother said. "A minor incident."

"Will one of you please tell me what happened?" I asked.

My mother gave Harvey a frustrated look and then said, "Oh, all right. Our sweet, elderly neighbor, Robert Jenkins, was out riding his bike this morning. He rides up and down the street several times each day to get some exercise. I was on my way home from the grocery store. As I rounded the corner ... well, I just, I didn't see him there, and I nicked him with my car."

"When you say you 'nicked him,' was he injured?" I asked.

"The bike got the worst of it. Robert has a few broken bones. He'll live."

Over the past year, I'd started to notice my mother's eyesight wasn't what it used to be. We'd all been pushing her to get her eyes checked. As much as I didn't like hearing about the accident she'd had earlier in the day, maybe it was the wakeup call she needed.

"Are you going to make an appointment for an eye exam?" I asked.

She rolled her eyes as if she'd expected the question and said, "Yes, dear. I already have. Now, can we *please* talk about something other than me?"

"We can," I said. "I had a couple of interesting visits today. The first was with Xander Thornton. He lost his wife not too long ago, and his brother is living with him, helping Xander with his daughter."

"Xander ... I believe he's the poor fellow Harvey told me had been tied to a tree in the park when he was younger, right?" my mother asked.

I nodded. "When I visited with him today he also admitted to prank-calling some of his female classmates when they were back in high school. When they answered, he'd breathe into the phone, say their names, that kind of thing."

Harvey set his fork down, running a hand along his jaw. "You think the kid did it? You think he killed his classmates to get revenge for what they did to him?"

"I don't know. I'll admit, he acted strange toward the end of the visit. We all know his father gave him an alibi all those years ago, but the man could have lied."

"Would have been good to question his pop a second time," Harvey said. "Too bad he's dead."

"Xander has the strongest motive of anyone I've questioned. If he's guilty, though, I haven't found the evidence I need to prove it yet."

"You said you had a couple of visits today," Whitlock said. "Who was the second?"

"Ty Conroy. He's a teacher now, like his dad had been. I got the impression he's dealing with some demons of his own. I'm just not sure if they're demons from the past or the present. When I walked into his classroom after school was over for the day, I caught him drinking out of a flask he keeps in his desk drawer."

"Maybe he was winding down after a long day," Whitlock said.

"I questioned him about the day he assaulted Jackson at school after the principal found out he'd given his father's biology exam to Jackson so he could pass the class."

"Seems like small potatoes to me," Whitlock said. "I never got the impression Ty had anything to do with what happened to those kids at the cabin."

"I agree with you. It was a petty high school squabble, the kind teenagers have all the time. I'd never assume someone would resort to murder over it, except for one thing."

"What's that?" Harvey asked.

"He made a comment while I was there, and it's been bugging me."

"Well ... go on," my mother said. "What did he say?"

"Ty's father took his own life a week after the incident."

"Drug overdose, as I recall," Harvey said.

"You're right. Ty told me his father stopped speaking to him after he learned about what Ty had done with his test questions. Did either of you know?"

Whitlock looked at Harvey. "I didn't. Did you?"

"Sure didn't," Harvey said. "Puts a new perspective on things, doesn't it?"

It did.

"Ty gave the test to Jackson, trusting him not to show it to anyone else. Not only did Jackson show it to the same group of friends who were murdered at the cabin, Ty's father died before Ty had a chance to smooth things over with him."

"Must have done a number on the kid," Whitlock said.

My mother aimed her fork in my direction, saying, "I don't know about you three, but I don't see it. Sure, the kid's father was angry. He didn't speak to his son, and then he took his own life, leaving his kid reeling about the choices he'd made. This is life. Family stops speaking to each other sometimes. It doesn't mean they go out and commit a bunch of murders."

"Oh, I don't know, Darlene," Whitlock said. "He may have wanted revenge, and revenge is just as good of a motive as any."

"Seems like a lot of phooey to me," my mother said. "The tree you're barking up, Georgiana. I'm sorry to say, I'm not so sure it's the right one."

Whitlock and Harvey went quiet, eyeing me as if waiting to see how I'd respond to the unsolicited advice I'd been given.

But I was fine with it.

She was just trying to help.

She also didn't know the first thing about criminals and how they operated.

Perhaps it was better to take the high road, to make her feel like she was part of the investigation, to make her feel seen, heard, and validated. She may have said she wanted to be involved with the case to keep an eye on Harvey, but I didn't believe it was the only reason. I'm sure it made her feel closer to me and the air in which I lived and breathed. It was a world she'd never been part of—a world I was sure she wanted to understand.

"I'm not sure who's to blame for the murders yet, but I'm working hard at it," I said.

And I was getting closer.

I could feel it.

I could also feel something else. No matter who I talked to, almost all roads seemed to lead back to the same person—Jackson.

29

I was relieved to be home after such a long day—a day that had left me with more questions than answers. I was sitting on the balcony, processing it all as I watched the moonlight flicker across the ocean's surface. It was calm and serene, the perfect way for me to relax beneath the warmth of my fluffy pink blanket.

Giovanni finished up in the kitchen and joined me, topping up my glass of pinot noir. Then he slid into the chair next to mine.

"You've been quieter than usual this evening," he said. "Do you want to tell me about your day?"

"I think I'd rather give it a rest tonight," I said. "My mind's filled with questions I don't have answers to yet, and I'm tired of thinking about the investigation."

"Is there anything I can do to help?"

"You can talk to me about anything other than the case I'm investigating."

Giovanni stood and walked over to the bar cart. He browsed the various options on the shelf and then grabbed a glass and a bottle of whiskey. He poured himself a double shot, took a sip, and returned to his seat, bottle in hand.

For a time, he didn't say a word, leading me to believe he had something on his mind. Whenever there was something serious to discuss, I'd noticed he'd hesitate at first, as if trying to figure out the right words to say.

Given any length of silence between two people made me anxious, I said, "Is there something you'd like to talk to me about?"

He turned toward me, smiling as he said, "You have a lot going on with the case. What I have to say can wait until after the investigation is over."

The care and consideration he'd always shown for my needs meant a lot to me. But at the moment, I needed to know what was on his mind.

"If there's something you want to talk to me about, let's talk about it," I said.

"Are you sure?"

"I am. When we got together, we agreed we wouldn't keep things from each other."

"I am not keeping anything from you."

"I'm not saying you are," I said. "You're just not telling me what's on your mind. Something's bothering you. I can tell."

"It's all right. I don't feel it's the right time. Let's wait until your mind is not occupied with other things."

Now I was even more curious.

And not just curious—worried.

What wasn't he telling me?

"I can't go to bed tonight knowing there's something you want to discuss with me. I need to know what's going on in that head of yours."

He reached over, pulling me next to him.

As he met my gaze, he said, "Your needs are far more important to me than my own. They always have been."

He was still hesitating.

"Talk to me," I said. "Please. Whatever it is ... let it out."

He wrapped his arms around me and said, "I proposed to you because I want us to be married."

"I know."

"Ever since my proposal, you haven't mentioned anything to me about our wedding. We haven't discussed when we should get married, or where, or even what kind of wedding you'd like to have. I feel it's important to ask ... Do you still want to get married?"

His question shocked me.

"Of course, I do," I said.

"It seems to me like you're holding back. Why haven't we started planning our future together?"

"We *are* planning our future. We're living it, right here, right now."

"Not as man and wife."

Since his proposal, I *hadn t* talked about the wedding. I supposed I thought we were in no rush because I wasn't in one. Reflecting on what he'd just said, I thought about the seriousness of the tone in his voice. Cementing plans for our future and choosing a date meant more to him than I'd realized. He'd been patient, waiting all this time for me to say something—anything—and I had said nothing.

"I'm sorry, Giovanni," I said. "I should have discussed it with you. Instead, I allowed life and all its complications to get in the way of us. I never meant to give you a reason to question my commitment to you. I *am* committed. You mean everything to me."

He kissed me on the forehead. "I want more than anything to be your husband."

He'd always been so good at sharing his feelings. It wasn't often I opened myself up enough to reach deep down inside to a place where I could sit in my rawest of emotions. I found myself in such a place now, at the core of my truth, reflecting on why I'd held back.

Here was a man like no other I'd been with before. A man deserving of everything I had to give—every word, every thought, every part of me. Over time, he'd stripped away the walls I'd so firmly put in place, leaving me vulnerable but also filled with a feeling of love that was more powerful than anything I'd ever known.

The pain I'd experienced in my past had bound me for far too long.

The death of my father.

The death of my daughter.

A failed marriage to another man.

The time had come to let it all go, to allow myself the peace and renewal that came with trusting again. Not just Giovanni. I needed to trust myself, my future ... *our* future.

"The truth is, I think I haven't talked about our future or setting a wedding date because part of me hasn't ever let go of my past, not all of it," I said.

"Is there anything I can do?"

"You just did. You see me, and you always have. You just made me realize I'd been hesitating this entire time. I should have talked to you."

"I'm glad we are now."

"I am too, and I don't want to wait. We've waited half of our adult lives to find each other again. Now that we have, let's plan our future, starting with our wedding. You're right. It's time."

30

I woke the next morning feeling more refreshed than I had in a long time. The talk I'd had the night before with Giovanni had ended with a decision to choose a wedding date and start making plans as soon as the investigation was over.

I dressed and was out the door by nine o'clock, motivated to make today one that would end with my questions being answered. First on the agenda was a visit to the medical examiner's office to see Silas.

I found him sitting at the table, bobbing his head up and down as he hovered over a breakfast platter that looked like it came from a fast-food joint. His usual big-hair-band music wasn't playing in the background, which I found odd until I saw the earbuds in his ears.

I waved a hand in front of him. He didn't see me, so I bent down until my face was a few inches in front of his. He jumped back, and we both started laughing.

He removed the earbuds and said, "Hi'ya stranger. I've been wondering when you'd show up."

"I wanted to stop by yesterday, but the day got away from me. Ever since this investigation started, I've been going nonstop."

"I know the feeling. This case is different than the others. It may be a cold case, but you know how I am when something falls into my lap. I'm as determined as you are to get to the bottom of it, no matter how many hours I have to put in. Guessin' you're here for an update."

"I am."

"Cool. You have any specific questions for me?"

"I do. During the original investigation, scrapings were taken from under Aidan's fingernails. Have you looked over those test results?"

"I have, and I've tested them again. Sorry to say, they're not a match to anyone in the system."

Too bad.

I was hoping for better news.

"What about the note left on Cora's windshield?" I asked.

"I used a ninhydrin treatment to check for any latent fingerprints that may have been left on the note. There weren't any. He may have been wearing gloves."

"Have you been out to the cabin yet?"

"I have. Not much luck there either. I mean, there were fingerprints all over the place, but the amount of time it would take to process them all ... well, it would take a while. Wish I had better news for ya."

"Yeah, me too."

I was hoping for something more, a clue to point me in the right direction. Looked like I wouldn't find any here.

"You have any suspects yet?" he asked.

"A few."

"Anyone stand out more than the others?"

"You know how it is with these cases. I always seem to stumble before I get to the truth."

"You always get there in the end. Hey, I'm not sure how much help it would be to you, but Foley dropped off a box of evidence from the old investigation. Wanna look through it while you're here?"

I nodded and walked with Silas to his office.

He pointed to a box sitting on top of a chair next to the printer and said, "There you go."

I slid some gloves on, approached the box, and lifted the lid. Reaching inside, I pulled out several evidence bags. As I looked at the labels, I came across samples of the clothes the teens had been wearing that day, along with other things like soil, fibers, and hair. I set them to the side, and something caught my eye—a small baggie at the bottom of the box. I grabbed it out and held it in front of me.

"They filled out information on the location, but there's no description on that one," Silas said.

The location information indicated the bag's contents were found in the soil next to Owen's body.

"They may not have known what it was when they bagged it, but I do," I said.

"You do?"

The bag contained two tiny gold fragments, which at first glance would be hard to identify. But given what I'd recently learned, I knew what I was looking at.

"They're pieces off of a gold chain," I said.

"How do you know?"

I told him about the gold chains the boys had been given, and my theory about them being removed from their necks after they were murdered.

If I was right, and I believed I was, the killer *had* taken Owen's chain, and he may have taken the others too.

But why?

31

I was sitting across the street from Ray and Valerie's house, hoping Ray would leave the house so I could speak to Valerie alone. At the three-hour mark, I started getting antsy. There was at least one more stop I wanted to make today, and I was beginning to wonder if I was wasting my time.

I'd passed the minutes checking in with Hunter and Simone and catching up with Foley. Hunter had found out some things about Ray's past. He had nothing before he met Valerie, and he worked minimum-wage jobs, never staying in any one position for long.

In my conversation with Foley, he let me know he'd tried calling Danny Donovan about an hour before, but Danny hadn't answered. He'd also tried Danny's sister, Dorothy, and got the same result. I wanted to believe the story Danny had told me, and I wanted to believe he was innocent. But the fact neither of them had answered their phones or returned their calls was suspect. Before the call ended, Foley let me know he was sending Whitlock to Danny's residence to check in.

As my concerns about Danny grew, I started second-guessing myself. Perhaps I'd been naïve, buying into the story he'd told me about stumbling across the bodies and being too afraid to talk to the police. If he *was* guilty, he'd done a good job of fooling me so far.

The day took a turn in my favor when I caught a glimpse of Ray walking out of the house, twirling a key ring around his fingers. He was dressed like he had a date with the gym. I watched him walk to his pickup, adjusting his rearview mirror after he hopped inside.

Although I'd lowered myself down in my seat, for a moment, I thought he'd seen me. He'd backed out of the driveway and was idling in the middle of the road for no apparent reason. He reached for what looked like a pack of gum, popped a piece in his mouth, and put the truck in drive.

After he rounded the corner, I waited a few minutes just in case he came back for some reason. When it appeared I was in the clear, I got out of the car.

No one came to the door when I knocked, but there was a vehicle in the driveway, suggesting someone was home.

Looking around, I spotted a doorbell.

I pressed the doorbell.

I waited.

Still nothing.

I debated about what to do next and decided to jiggle the door handle, surprised to find it was unlocked. I considered my options and decided to open the door, poking my head inside as I said, "Valerie, are you here?"

If she was there, she didn't respond, and if Ray was headed to the gym, and he came home afterward, I didn't have long.

I had a decision to make, and I made it.

I'd just stepped inside the house when I spotted a woman coming down the hallway. She was dressed in a robe and had a towel wrapped around her head.

She saw me, and she screamed.

I didn't blame her.

I was an intruder in her house.

As she turned and ran in the opposite direction, I shouted, "Valerie, I'm sorry I entered the house without your permission. I knocked, and I rang the doorbell. When no one came to the door, I realized it was unlocked, and I came inside. I should have waited."

A door slammed at the end of the hall.

I remained where I was and tried again.

"My name is Georgiana Germaine. I'm a private investigator working on your son's case. My associate, Simone, visited with you and your husband the other day. I have some followup questions, and I was hoping we could talk for a few minutes."

I waited one minute, then two.

The bedroom door remained closed.

I wondered if she'd texted Ray, telling him I was in the house.

As much as I wanted to stay, I needed to get out of there.

"Listen, Valerie ... again, I'm sorry," I said. "I'm going to head out, but before I do, there's one thing I want to say. I've learned something as I've been investigating this case. It's what I came to talk to you about. When Jackson was alive, one of his classmates thought he was being abused. She tried talking to him about it, but he wouldn't say anything. I was hoping you might know something about that. Anyway, I'm leaving now."

My opportunity to speak to Jackson's mother had been dashed thanks to my impulsive nature. I left the house feeling deflated, the opposite of how I'd felt that morning.

I was halfway back to my car when I heard, "Georgiana, wait."

I turned to see Valerie standing in the doorway.

"I don't have much time," she said. "I can't talk about Jackson when Ray is home."

I got right to it. "At the cabin, I noticed some items placed around the area where Jackson died. Someone left a football. It looks new."

"It was me. I visit as often as I can. I go to his grave too. It's just, that spot at the cabin, it's where he took his last breath."

"I'm glad you honor his memory," I said.

"If you want to speak to me, you should come inside now."

"Does Ray know I'm here? I guess what I'm asking is, when you shut yourself in the bedroom, did you text or call anyone?"

"I didn't."

I had a second chance, and I was determined not to mess it up this time.

I crossed the street, entering the house and following Valerie into a sitting room. She looked at the time and went quiet, as if doing calculations in her head.

"Okay, so ... he left about ten minutes ago. Takes about five minutes to get to the gym. His spin class is about an hour. You need to be quick."

Quick didn't allow me time to ease into my questions.

But assuming she'd heard what I'd been shouting before, she knew the nature of my visit.

What I wanted to talk about was the bruise over her left eye, but that could wait, for now.

"Do you have any reason to believe your son was being abused when he was alive?" I asked.

"When you say *abused,* what type of abuse are you talking about and what proof do you have?"

"The girl Jackson was dating, Aubree, she told Cora she'd seen bruises on Jackson's shoulders and back."

Valerie began shaking her head.

"No," she said. "There's no way. I don't believe it. Ray ... he, he wouldn't have done anything to hurt Jackson."

I'd said Aubree thought Jackson was being abused.

I *hadn't* said anything about *Ray* being his abuser.

"Why did you mention Ray just now?" I asked.

"Umm ... no reason."

"There is a reason. What is it?"

"No, I can't."

"Can't what? Can't admit Ray abuses you, and may have also been abusing Jackson too when he was alive?"

"I was a good mother, you know. I tried to be."

"I'm sure you were. I bet when Ray was abusive to you back then, you believed if he took all his anger out on you, he wouldn't touch your son."

As the tears began to flow, she clasped a hand to her mouth. "Ray ... he's not a bad man. You don't know him."

She'd all but admitted the abuse.

I'd just told her Jackson may have suffered the same abuse.

And yet, she still defended him.

"I don't need to know Ray to know his type," I said.

"It's not what you think. It doesn't happen often. He loves me. He just loses his temper sometimes."

"I suppose that explains the shiner on your left eye?"

Valerie touched the bruised area. "It's nothing."

"Anger in any form of aggression is abuse, Valerie. It's not love. You don't hurt the ones you love. Physical abuse is a sign of selfishness, a sign of ownership, a sign of disrespect. I know how hard it can be to stand up for yourself. Maybe you don't want to, or maybe you don't because you love him. I bet it's easier to keep telling yourself he loves you than it is to face the truth."

She staggered backward, leaning against the wall, sobbing.

I said nothing for a few minutes, giving Valerie the chance to process what had already been said. But time was not on my side.

"Can I ask you a question?" I asked. "Did Jackson know you were being abused?"

"He didn't. I did everything I could to keep it from him."

"Assuming Jackson was abused, do you think it's possible he allowed it to go on because he thought the same way you did? Maybe he allowed it because Ray said if he did, he'd leave you alone."

"Ray wouldn't do that. He wouldn't have hurt Jackson. He just wouldn't. Believe what you like, but he loves me."

I crossed my arms, knowing what I needed to say next would sting even more.

"I believe Ray has been using you to get ahead in life," I said. "Your father's business was supposed to go to your son, and if not to him, then to be managed by you. I'm guessing Ray runs the show. Doesn't he? Seems convenient, like it just fell into his lap. Makes me wonder ... a guy like Ray, I bet he'd do whatever he had to in order to get ahead."

Valerie narrowed her eyes, staring at me in disbelief. "What are you saying? You're not ... you couldn't be suggesting Ray had anything to do with what happened to those kids?"

"I'm not suggesting anything. I'm just stating the obvious."

"Ray has a temper at times, but murder? He'd never kill anyone, let alone a group of teens."

She'd been brainwashed for so long, I wasn't even sure she knew the man she was married to or what he was capable of doing. And I wouldn't know either, not until I had the chance to speak to him.

"I'll tell you what Ray loves," I said. "He loves the life you provide him. You're his ticket to ride, his gravy train."

"Stop it! Stop saying things you don't know anything about."

"I'm not trying to upset you, Valerie. I'm trying to make you think. I asked one of my associates to look into Ray's past. Ray came from nothing. His family was poor. Before he met you, he worked minimum-wage jobs, and even then, he never stayed in any one position for long."

"Who cares about his past? I don't. I-I want you to leave."

"I know you want me to go before Ray gets home, but maybe I should stay and talk to him. I don't need to mention the abuse or the fact I know about it."

"No, you need to leave. You need to leave now."

I stood a moment, trying to decide my next move.

I decided to respect her wishes and allow time for the conversation we'd had to sink in.

"I'll leave," I said. "But I'd like to say one last thing before I go."

Valerie rolled her eyes and said, "Fine, make it quick."

"Abuse of any kind is never acceptable. I'm just a phone call away. You don't have to do this on your own. I want you to think about that and to think about your son. You may not have known Jackson was being abused back then, but you know now. The question is ... what are you going to do about it?"

32

"I figured you'd be back," Xander said. "I just didn't think it would be so soon."

I peered over his shoulder, looking to see if anyone else was home. "Are you alone?" I asked.

He nodded. "My daughter is playing at a friend's house, and my brother is at divorce mediation with his soon-to-be ex-wife."

"Can I come in? I'd like to continue the conversation we started yesterday."

"Why? Has something changed?"

"I just have a few followup questions for you," I said.

Xander stood there a moment and then shrugged. "Guess it would be all right."

We walked to the living room, and I sat down.

"You want some water or a soda or something?" he asked.

"No, I'm good."

"All right. I'll be right back."

The thought of Xander leaving the room without telling me why raised suspicion. He was at the top of my list of suspects. Still, getting him alone was a good thing. I hoped it would give me the opportunity to get him to say something he hadn't before, an admission or maybe even a confession.

While I waited for him to return, I kept one hand in my lap and the other beneath my shirt, palming my gun in the event I needed to use it.

Xander returned to the living room with a soda in hand. He plopped down on a chair, cracked the can open, and began gulping it down until it was gone. He set the empty can on the side table and looked at me. "Well, let's get to it. What are these followup questions of yours?"

"I've been thinking a lot about how you were treated when you were in high school," I said.

"What about it?"

"I'm sure you wanted what every teenager wanted at that age ... to be accepted. It's too bad Jackson and his friends messed with you the way they did."

"They didn't *all* mess with me. Owen was nice. So was Cora ... most of the time."

"What do you mean by *most* of the time?" I asked.

"Not that it matters, but I had a crush on her for a while."

"Did she know?"

"I think so. I said as much to her once."

"What did she say?"

"She told me she wasn't looking for a relationship, but then I started to notice the way she looked at Owen. It wasn't the way a person looked at a friend. It was the way a person looked at someone they liked."

"So she lied to you," I said.

"I wouldn't say she lied. I'd say she didn't feel the same about me as I felt about her, and she let me down easy."

Owen and Cora seemed different than the rest of the group. They hadn't teased or taunted Xander like the others had. But if he had a crush on Cora, it made me wonder if jealousy had played a part in his feelings toward her.

"Do you remember some of the football players wearing gold chains back then?" I asked.

Xander tapped a finger on the arm of the chair, thinking. "Don't think so. Why?"

"The football coach gave them to the star players, which would have included Owen, Aidan, and Jackson."

"What about them?"

"I was looking at a piece of evidence today that had been collected at the crime scene. I don't think the detectives knew what it was when they found it, but I believe it was a couple of links from one of the gold chains the boys were given."

"Okayyy. Why tell me about it?"

I looked him in the eye. "I'm telling you because I think at least one of the boys was wearing the chain they'd been given on the day they died. Strange thing is, in the crime scene photos, the boys weren't wearing them."

"So ...?"

I'd brought up the gold chains to gauge his reaction, which seemed apathetic. Maybe he was telling me the truth. Maybe Owen had been wearing the necklace on the day he died, and when he was assaulted, it had fallen off or broken. Maybe my theory was just that —a theory.

"I'd like to know more about your home life back then," I said. "Would you say it was normal?"

"I'd say it was decent. My dad did the best he could."

"I heard you may have been held back in school."

"Yeah, it's true. I was held back for two years. It was embarrassing, trying to fit in, knowing the rumors being spread about me. Everyone thought I was stupid. I wasn't stupid. It just took me longer to learn things than it did for other people."

I was pleased with our conversation so far.

He was opening up, responding to my questions without any pushback.

"Back when I was in school, when there was a student who

seemed different than everyone else, we didn't understand it like we do today," I said.

"You're around my age, aren't you?"

"I'm older than you are. I turned forty-seven this year."

Xander slapped a hand to his knee and said, "Whoa, you don't look a day over forty."

I appreciated the compliment.

"What I was trying to say before is that when I was in school, we didn't speak about personality disorders the way we do today," I said. "If we had, maybe the kids we went to school with would have been a lot more understanding of each other."

"Maybe. What are you getting at?"

"You may not want to admit it, even now, but I bet you were angry about the way you were treated in school."

He blinked at me, a wry grin forming on his lips as he said, "Angry enough to kill? It's why you're here again so soon, isn't it? Are you looking for a confession? Do you think I killed them?"

"I'm not sure."

"Be straight with me. I can take it."

He said he could take it, but I wasn't sure he could.

"All right," I said. "Out of everyone I've looked at and talked to during my investigation, no one had a bigger motive to commit the murders than you did."

Xander shook his head. "You have balls, I'll give you that. You come into my house, and you admit I'm the one you think committed the murders."

"I said you have motive. I didn't say you did it."

"You don't have to say it. You want it to be me. I can tell by the way you're talking to me. What if I did murder my classmates? What if you're right? Do you feel safe now, alone in the house with me?"

The conversation was going in a direction I hadn't expected. I didn't know what to make of it. Was he teasing me in some way by not admitting to the murders outright?

"Are you offering to tell me the truth?" I asked.

Xander smiled and burst out laughing. "I had you going for a minute, didn't I? Of course I didn't do it. I was just riling you up."

"It's not a joking matter."

"I know it isn't. Can you blame me? Between yesterday and today, our conversations have been so heavy, I felt the need to lighten things up, even for a few minutes. I hope you catch the guy you're after, I mean it. Those guys didn't always show me kindness when we were in school, but they didn't deserve to die."

In some ways, it felt like we were playing a game, much like the game he'd played with Aubree. Speaking of…

"What made you decide to play the word game with Aubree?" I asked. "You must have known there was a chance she'd discover your identity."

"I felt guilty about the calls. I knew it wasn't right not to tell them who I was when we were talking. When Aubree pushed me to give her my name, I thought it might be time to come clean. I knew there would be consequences."

"Consequences, yes. But I can't imagine you thought it would lead to what happened in the park. You didn't tell the police who assaulted you in the park that day. I still don't understand why."

"Those guys were just trying to stand up for their girls by making me pay for how I'd made them feel. I didn't know they were as scared as they were. In the park that night, Aubree told me how it made her feel. She was crying. I'll never forget it. I guess I thought I deserved what they did to me, so I kept quiet."

"You attended the funerals of everyone who died at the cabin, and I heard you were emotional. Why?"

"Same reason as everyone else, I guess. Funerals bring it out in people."

He had a plausible answer for every question I'd thrown at him so far.

But did I believe his answers?

I didn't know.

I couldn't stop thinking about the way he'd been joking with me minutes before. Jokes often had some basis in truth and were driven by honest emotion.

How much truth were in his?

As I sat there, deep in thought, he stood and said, "After Owen heard about what happened to me in the park, he wrote me a note. It wasn't long, just a few lines. I think it's with some of the other things I kept from back then. Want to see it?"

"Sure."

He walked down the hall, whistling. A minute later, I heard what sounded like someone shuffling through drawers.

Once again, my nerves were getting the better of me.

He'd said he'd go find the note, but he could have been doing anything.

And then the whistling stopped.

And the house went quiet.

Too quiet.

"Xander, you all right back there?" I asked.

There was no response, which had me creating various scenarios in my head, none of which were good.

"Xander, did you hear me?" I asked. "Want some help finding the note?"

Seconds went by, and then I heard movement.

I gripped my gun, prepared for anything when he came around the corner. But nothing could have prepared me for what I saw when he came into view.

I raised my gun, aiming it at him. "Don't move, and don't come any closer. Put your hands up, Xander."

He shook his head and said, "You don't understand. It's not what you think."

33

"*It's not what I think?*" I asked. "You're holding a gold chain in your hand."

Xander looked at the chain and then back at me. "You can put the gun away. I don't know how it ended up here. I promise."

He took a step toward me.

"Don't move," I said.

"I was just ... I was going to give it to you."

"Stay where you are. If you want to give it to someone, you can give it to the police when they get here."

"The police? No, no, no. We don't need any police. We just need to talk, to—"

Outside, I heard what sounded like a vehicle turning into the driveway.

It wasn't the police.

No one knew I was here.

Xander turned, looking over his shoulder as he said, "Marcus is home."

Marcus.

My mind was a flurry of emotions, thoughts entering and exiting all at once.

And then clarity came.

A decision needed to be made, and fast.

I hid the gun back beneath my shirt.

"Where did you find that chain?" I asked.

"In the spare bedroom Marcus has been staying in. I was looking through the drawers for a box where I keep some of my old high school memorabilia, and I ... I ..."

"You what?"

Xander's eyes widened.

"No, it can't be true," he said. "It can't be. He wouldn't have ..."

Except he did.

"You understand what this means, don't you?" I asked.

Xander started panting like he was struggling to catch his breath, and he said, "You need to leave. Right now. Hurry. You can go out the back door. Maybe he won't see your car parked across the street."

"I'm staying."

"You can't. It's not safe. He and I, we need to talk. I need to understand. You gotta get out of here."

The front door opened, and Marcus came inside.

Xander made a fist, attempting to conceal the chain in his hand.

Marcus looked at Xander and then at me. "Well, well, nice seeing you again, Detective. What brings you by today?"

Xander cleared his throat and said, "The ... ahh, the detective stopped by to ask me a few more questions. Nothing major."

Marcus' eyes narrowed into tiny slits. "You know something, little brother ... you've never been a good liar."

"I'm not lying. The detective was just leaving."

Marcus moved his hands to his hips, grunting out a laugh. "Why leave? Stay a while. I'll make dinner, and we can all talk. Seems to me like we have a lot to talk about, wouldn't you say? We can start with the gold chain you're hiding from me."

There was no sense lying about it now.

Marcus had seen it already.

Not that I minded.

If Marcus wanted to get it all out in the open, I was happy to oblige.

I was happy to shoot him too ... I just needed a reason, and I hoped he'd give me one. After what he'd done, it was the least I could do.

"Xander found a gold chain in the guest room," I said. "The same room you're staying in, Marcus. Care to explain?"

Marcus ran a hand along his chin. "Well now, I wouldn't know. Have you asked Xander? It's his house, and that room is filled with his stuff. I'd say he has some explaining to do."

"*I* have some explaining to do?" Xander asked. "I'd say *you* have some explaining to do."

"Don't be coy, brother. Why are you holding out on us?"

"Let me make it clear for you, Marcus," I said. "Jackson, Aidan, and Owen were given gold chains by their football coach. Pieces of a gold chain were found at the crime scene. I saw them this morning when I stopped by to talk to the medical examiner. Care to know what else we spoke about? Aidan had skin cells beneath his fingernails."

"Blah, blah, blah," Marcus said. "Get to the flipping point."

"When the murders were committed, the skin cells weren't a match to anyone in the database. But skin cells contain DNA, as I'm sure you know. If I suspect someone of those murders, and the police get a warrant for said person, we could test that person's DNA against the DNA collected twenty years ago. Take a minute to think about that ... let it marinate. I'll wait."

Xander turned toward me, his voice strained as he said, "I had no idea the chain was even there until a few minutes ago. I swear."

"I believe you," I said.

Marcus clapped his hands together. "Well, isn't that sweet? What do you suppose we do now?"

I lifted my shirt, showing Marcus the gun I had aimed at his chest.

"Hands up, Marcus," I said.

"Hands up ... or what?"

"Xander, call the police," I said.

"He will do no such thing," Marcus said. "He's a softie. He'd need a backbone to do that, and he's never had one."

"Call the police, Xander," I repeated.

Xander wiped his brow and said, "I ... uhh ... I don't know ... I ..."

"There's only one play here," I said. "There's no point defending your brother. He wasn't going to defend you. Didn't you hear what he just said? He was trying to blame you, to make it seem like *you're* the guilty one, not him."

"Don't listen to her," Marcus said.

"Both of you, be quiet!" Xander said. "I need to think."

"There's nothing to think about," Marcus said. "We can solve this little predicament we've gotten ourselves into here and now. We can make it all go away."

"She has a gun," Xander said.

"So what?" Marcus scoffed. "A gun's nothing if a person isn't prepared to use it."

"Give me a reason," I said. "I've been waiting for one."

"Tough words for a little lady in a flirty little skirt," Marcus said. "You expect us to believe you're woman enough to pull the trigger? Because I don't."

"Tell me something ... why keep the gold chain and why bring it here, to your brother's house?"

Marcus turned toward Xander and said, "I bet we can get to her before she gets a shot off. What do you say?"

"No," Xander said. "We're not going to hurt her. We're going to let her go."

"Just how stupid are you?" Marcus shouted. "We can't let her go. I mean, we could have, but you had to go and show her the chain. This is *your* fault. *Your* mess. You need to clean it up now for both of us."

His speech was so convincing, it almost deserved a round of applause.

Almost.

"Your acting performance yesterday, pretending like you had no idea your brother was being bullied when he was in school," I said. "Well done."

"Oh, I knew, and I knew all about what happened in the park. Dad told me. Took him hours to get Xander to admit who'd done it to him."

"If your dad knew who was involved, why didn't he tell the police?" I asked.

"My dad was the type of person who felt it was best to take matters into our own hands, if you know what I mean. He didn't think I'd take it as far as I did, of course."

A tear rolled down Xander's cheek.

He brushed it away and said, "How could you, Marcus?"

"Don't shed a tear for those brats," Marcus said. "Those kids deserved what happened to them. Sometimes an example needs to be made, consequences paid. Ask me, what I did ... it was justified."

Xander's classmates may have thought Xander had a few screws loose, but the loose screw wasn't Xander, it was Marcus.

"They were my friends," Xander said.

"They weren't your friends. They hated you. They made fun of you. They made everyone in school see you as a chump, someone they could do whatever they wanted to because you didn't have what it took to stand up for yourself."

Marcus shot me a wink and then took a step in my direction, testing my resolve. I welcomed it.

"Take one more step, and I will shoot you," I said.

"Hold on a minute," Xander said. "No one needs to shoot anybody. We can work this out."

"No more small talk," Marcus said. "This ends now."

Xander faced his brother. "I won't let you hurt anyone else."

"Suit yourself," Marcus said. "All these years, you haven't changed a bit. It's just like always ... if something needs to be done, I have to do it myself."

Marcus lunged for the gun.

Xander reached for his brother.

And I fired.

34

"Nice work," Foley said.

"I wouldn't say I solved the case like I usually do," I said. "I just happened to be here when Xander discovered the gold chain in his guest room drawer. I should have known it was Marcus after he went out of his way to lie to me yesterday."

"I have no doubt you would have figured it out. Give yourself more credit. This case wasn't solved in twenty years, and you cracked it in less than a week."

I may have, but it wasn't like my other cases.

I wasn't used to a case resolving itself before I figured it out.

I'd shot Marcus in the abdomen. It was enough to put him down, but not enough to kill him, which was my intention. And it couldn't have happened at a more perfect moment. In Marcus' wallet, Whitlock found another note we were sure was meant for Cora. The note suggested she should "watch her back," even though he told the police the note was meant to scare her, nothing more.

I didn't believe it.

None of us did.

Xander was shaken up, but once he calmed down enough to talk, the mystery of the gold chain and how it came to be in the dresser drawer revealed itself.

A few days earlier, Marcus' ex had packed up some of his things, telling him he needed to come by and get them or she was taking it all to the landfill. She'd come across the piece of jewelry in his nightstand and had thrown it into a shoebox with a handful of other items. Marcus hadn't even realized it was in there.

As Xander was in the guest room, looking for the note Owen had written, he'd moved the box to the side, and the lid came off, revealing the chain inside. It may have been two decades, but once he saw it, he remembered seeing the chains around some of the footballers' necks.

To say nothing or tell the truth, knowing what would happen to his brother if he did. He thought of Cora, and the feelings he'd had for her at one time.

Today, honesty had prevailed.

As I stood next to Whitlock watching Marcus being wheeled past on a stretcher, I had one last dig to get in. I leaned down as he went by, smiling as I whispered, "Who's woman enough now, you little prick?"

I watched Marcus being loaded into the ambulance and then I called Cora. She was relieved to know the killer was in custody at last. No longer did she need to look over her shoulder or avoid a town she once called home. She was free, as free as one could be, given what she'd been through in life.

"I heard you couldn't get ahold of Danny earlier today," I said to Whitlock. "Not that it matters. No need to keep tabs on him now."

"He was out fishing with his sister," Whitlock said. "Left their cell phones in the car. Guessing we better get Harvey on the horn, give him the good news."

"Do you want to call him or shall I?"

"You cracked it. You make the call."

I took out my cell phone and then hesitated when a call came into the work line. After hours, all calls coming into the office forwarded to me. On any other day, I wouldn't have answered, but today, something told me I should.

I answered the call and was met with a single word, "Help."

Then the line went dead.

Whitlock took one look at my face and said, "What is it? What's wrong?"

"I can't be sure, but I think I may have just received a call from Valerie. She's Jackson's mother."

"What's happened?"

"I don't know, but I don't think it's good."

As we raced to my car, I gave Whitlock a quick recap of my visit with Valerie that morning. He grabbed the passenger-side door handle and said, "I'm coming with you."

Ten minutes later, we parked in front of Ray and Valerie's house and sprinted to the front door, which we found ajar. Inside, we heard someone crying, and not just crying—wailing.

We drew our guns and nodded at one another, creeping inside the house and following the sounds to the kitchen, where we found Valerie on the floor, hovering over Ray. Blood was everywhere. On the walls. On the tile floor. On his clothing. On hers.

"What happened, Valerie?" I asked.

"It's Ray ... he's ahh ... he's dead," she managed to choke out.

Whitlock tapped me on my shoulder, and I looked up, spotting an elderly gentleman bending over a chair in the living room. He, too, was bleeding, but he was alive. His hand was pressed against his left breast.

I looked at Whitlock. "There's a first aid kit in my car. Grab it for me and call 9-1-1."

"Roger that," he said.

I rushed to the older gentleman's side and said, "Sir, help is on the way. Until then, we'll do our best to stop the bleeding."

He nodded and said, "My name is Hugo. I am Valerie's father."

"What happened here?"

"You the detective who was here earlier today?" Hugo asked.

"I am."

"After you left the house, my daughter called me. She told me what you said, and I came straight over. She was catching me up on her life, and that's when she told me about the abuse. And I ... I ..."

Tears gushed down his face like a flooded dam after a heavy rainstorm.

"Take a breath for me, Hugo," I said.

Another nod, and a deep breath in.

"He came home, you see, and I confronted him," Hugo said. "I'll be honest, I wanted to wrap my hands around the guy's neck and squeeze the life out of him."

"How did he die?" I asked.

"The three of us were all standing in the kitchen, arguing ... well, more like yelling at each other. I told him he was finished—at the dealership, with my daughter ... it was over. I told him everyone would soon know what he did, and I'd make sure no one within a hundred miles from here would ever hire a scumbag like him."

Whitlock returned, and we opened the first aid kit, pulling out what we needed to treat Hugo's wound until the ambulance arrived, which I expected wouldn't be long. If I was going to find out how Ray died, I had to do it now.

As I dressed his wound, I said, "You didn't tell me how Ray died."

"All of this ... the house, his job, the car he drives, it's all in my name. When he realized he was going to lose it all, he grabbed a knife out of the block on the counter, and he stabbed me. Good thing the sucker had poor aim."

It was a good thing.

But it failed to explain how Ray was dead and Hugo was alive.

"What happened next?"

"He was getting ready to stab me a second time, and I beat him to it. Grabbed a knife and plunged it in where I knew it would do the most damage. When I was younger, back before I got into the auto business, I trained to be a doctor, you see. But I realized it wasn't for me. Learned a lot, though, and today, I'd say that training came in handy."

I glanced at Valerie, who was staring at her father, but still hadn't said a word.

"Valerie, do you have anything to add?" I asked.

"I ... ahh ... I ..."

"She doesn't," Hugo said. "My daughter has been through a lot. What do you say we save any further questions until later?"

"Later, meaning, until after you've had the chance to consult with your lawyer," I said.

Hugo grinned. "Something like that."

The whine of the ambulance could be heard speeding up the road. It wasn't long before the house was teeming with police. By then, Hugo's lawyer had arrived, and I had a feeling his version of the story would stick.

As I stood outside with Whitlock, I asked myself why Valerie had called me and why she had asked for help. I assumed she was in shock when her father was stabbed and hadn't realized his knife wound wasn't fatal at first. In her desperation, she didn't know who to turn to, so she'd called me.

Hugo could have stabbed Ray like he said he did, but something in Valerie's eyes when I looked at her told me his version of the story wasn't an accurate one.

"A penny for a thought," Whitlock said. "What do you say?"

"I've been thinking about Hugo's story and whether his version of events is the truth."

"And what have you decided?"

"After giving it some thought, I've decided it is the version I choose to believe."

I would tell the same version of the story to Foley and anyone else who asked me. As far as I was concerned, justice had been served, not once, but twice today.

THE END

Thank you for reading Little Stolen Memories, book nine in the *USA Today* bestselling Georgiana Germaine mystery series.

I hope you enjoyed getting to know the characters in this story as much as I have enjoyed writing them for you. This is a continuing series with more books coming before and after the one you just read. You can find the series order (as of the date of this printing) in the "Books by Cheryl Bradshaw" section below.

In Little Empty Promises, book ten in the series:

How far would you go to protect your secret?

As the sun sets over the quaint town of Cambria, California, Cordelia Bennett, a sprightly seventy-two-year-old librarian, hums a classic tune while tidying up the bookshelves.
Just as she's about to lock up for the night, a mysterious sound startles her. She turns. The fading light reveals a chilling presence in the shadows, and Cordelia realizes she's not alone.
Someone else is there, watching her every move—someone with one agenda in mind—making sure today is Cordelia's last.

What Readers are Saying about the Series:
"Makes you want to keep reading the story into the night."
"A strong lead character and plenty of drama, it keeps the reader engaged."
"Leaving you wanting to read more."
"You feel like you live close by and can see these characters walking by and waving to you."
"I will definitely read more from this author."
"Kept me on the edge of my seat."

Want a sneak peek? Here's an exclusive look at chapter one ...

LITTLE EMPTY PROMISES

1

It was a rather cool day in the sleepy town of Cambria, California, the brisk frigidity of fall sweeping through the streets like snow's first drift. Seventy-one-year-old Cordelia Bennett walked up and down the aisles of the local library, feather duster in hand, humming to the tune of Neil Young's "Heart of Gold." It was her fourth day as a library volunteer, and she was grateful for the opportunity. It whisked her away from the quiet of home, a home that held an abundance of bittersweet memories.

One year earlier, Cordelia's husband Marlon had passed away, dashing the plans they'd made to spend their golden years cruising around the world. His death had been sudden and unexpected, leaving her in a state of grief. He'd always been her lifeline, her confidant, the one person who had always made her safe.

She couldn't travel now.

Not without her trusted companion.

It wouldn't be the same.

Nothing would ever be the same again.

Tonight was the first time Cordelia was to close the library on her own, and it was of the utmost importance that everything went to plan. The book drop had been emptied, book returns had been checked in and reshelved, paper had been added to the photocopier and fax machine, and all laptops had been turned off and plugged in for recharging.

As Cordelia did her final rounds, she ran the feather duster along one of the bookshelves, pausing a moment to ingest a lungful of air. Holding the breath a moment, she savored a specific aroma, an aroma only timeless, weathered books could provide. The scent had always reminded her of the subtle fragrance of a candle—earthy with a slight dash of vanilla.

Pleased she'd checked everything off her list, Cordelia grabbed her handbag out of the cubby in the back room and made her way to the front door, stopping to switch off the lights. The sound of what Cordelia imagined was a book falling from one of the shelves startled her. She stood a moment in silence, trying to pinpoint which direction it came from, but the room had returned to silence. Cordelia went aisle to aisle, scanning the floor for any signs of book, but nothing, it seemed, had come off the shelves.

How odd.
If it isn't a book, what was it?
Taking the inspection a bit further, Cordelia moved to the reading area, thinking she may have overlooked a book left on one of the tables or chairs.

She found nothing.

She walked to the front desk, scanning the counter and the floor around it.

All was in order.
And then she heard something else.
A different sound this time.
Not of something falling.
A sound like ... footsteps.
It couldn't be.

She was alone in the library.

Cordelia had been sure to lock the doors of the library after the last person departed. Then she'd checked the handle, ensuring the door was locked.

The moon's light filtered through the window, and Cordelia froze. She could have sworn she'd seen movement on the opposite side of the room. But had she?

"Hello?" she asked. "Is anyone there?"

She'd asked as more of a formality, believing her mind was playing tricks on her, until a shadowy figure stepped out from behind a bookcase.

Stunned, Cordelia said, "You can't be here. The library is closed now. It opens at nine if you wish to return. Come along. I'll let you out."

But the figure didn't "come along," as she'd suggested. The figure remained motionless, confusing Cordelia even more. A thought ran through her mind. It was possible she was dealing with a homeless individual who had nowhere to go and, as such, had decided to seek refuge for the evening.

"Excuse me," Cordelia said. "Is there a reason you are refusing to leave? Do you have anywhere else you can go?"

She hoped for an answer this time, but once again, she was met with silence.

A second thought presented itself, one Cordelia didn't want to entertain. It was enough to make her reach into her handbag, taking her time as she fumbled around, her hand coming to land on a gun. It was the tiniest of things, a gift from Marlon. She'd scoffed when he'd given it to her years before, saying she had no use for a firearm.

Upon bestowing it to her, Marlon had said, "If the need should ever arise, all you have to remember is to point and shoot, dear."

The need had never arisen—until now.

And what's more, the gun had never been fired before.

Cordelia didn't even know what would happen if she tried.

Hands shaking, she raised the gun in front of her, searching for the words she wanted to say.

"I don't know who you are or why you're here, but I'm leaving now," she said.

"You're not going anywhere."

The words had been grunted in such a way to make Cordelia believe the person she was dealing with was going through great effort to mask his voice.

"Like I said, I'm leaving," Cordelia said. "You should do the same."

"What did you see?"

"I beg your pardon?"

"What. Did. You. See?"

"I'm not sure what you're talking about. What did I see ... when?"

"You *know* when."

"I'm afraid not."

"What did you see *here*, in the library?"

"I see lots of things each day. Can you be more specific?"

"Stop toying with me."

"I can assure you, there's no *toying* involved." There was a click, a sound that made Cordelia fear she wasn't the only one holding a gun. "You should know, I'm armed."

"Makes two of us."

"I'm not afraid to fire, if necessary. Though I'd rather not."

"It's too late."

Too late for what?

With the door to the library locked, Cordelia would have to turn her back on the man to unlock it, a measure too risky to take.

"I see we're at an impasse," she said. "I don't know what I saw or why it's too late. Can we agree to disagree and call it a night?"

"We can call it a night *after* you're dead."

Cordelia replayed the words in her mind a few times, her heart racing as she found herself out of ideas and with nowhere to turn.

"Do you think I'm afraid to die?" she asked. "I'm not."

It was a half-truth at best, but she was hoping to appeal to the intruder's humanity.

Maybe if she could do that, there was still a way out.

"Ever since my husband died, I've been a shell of the person," she added. "He was my everything. I lived to breathe the air around him. I miss the sound of his voice, the way his smile brightened the darkest of days. And his smell ... I sit in his car sometimes just so I can be reminded of it. Without him, I've struggled to find my way forward. But I believe even in our darkest of days, there is always a way forward. Wouldn't you agree?"

It was quiet for some time, and then there was a loud popping sound, followed by a pain ... a stabbing pain in Cordelia's chest.

She sagged to the ground, clutching her heart as she whispered, "I'll be seeing you, Marlon. I'll be seeing you soon."

I hope you enjoyed the sneak peek!

Reserve your copy of Little Empty Promises today at CherylBradshawStore.Com

Enjoy Little Stolen Memories?

You can show your appreciation by leaving a review on Amazon, Barnes & Noble, Apple Books, Google Play, Kobo, or Goodreads.

If you write a review, please be sure to email Cheryl (cheryl@authorcherylbradshaw.com) so she can express her gratitude. She does her best to reply to as many emails as she can, and she appreciates every piece of mail she receives.

About Cheryl Bradshaw

Cheryl Bradshaw is a New York Times and 11-time USA Today bestselling author writing in multiple genres, including mystery, thriller, romantic suspense, supernatural suspense, and poetry. She is a Shamus Award finalist for best private eye novel of the year, an eFestival of Words winner for best thriller, and has published over fifty books since 2011.

When she's not writing, Cheryl loves jet-setting to new countries, playing with her grandkids, high tea, and pursuing a wishful side career as a professional food tester of wine and cheese.

Never Miss One of Cheryl's Book's Again!

Sign up for Cheryl Bradshaw's "Killer Newsletter" today to be the first to know when a new book is released and to enter to win fun bookish swag. You'll also receive some fantastic book freebies just for joining!

Learn more by visiting her website at CherylBradshaw.Com

BOOKS BY CHERYL BRADSHAW

Sloane Monroe Series

Silent as the Grave (Prequel, Book 0)
When the body of Rebecca Barlow is found floating in the lake, private investigator Sloane Monroe takes on her very first homicide.

Black Diamond Death (Book 1)
Charlotte Halliwell has a secret. But before revealing it to her sister, she's found dead.

Murder in Mind (Book 2)
A woman is found murdered, the serial killer's trademark "S" carved into her wrist.

I Have a Secret (Book 3)
Doug Ward has been running from his past for twenty years. But after his fourth whisky of the night, he doesn't want to keep quiet, not anymore.

Stranger in Town (Book 4)
A frantic mother runs down the aisles, searching for her missing daughter. But little Olivia is already gone.

Bed of Bones (Book 5) (USA Today Bestselling Book)
Sometimes even the deepest, darkest secrets find their way to the surface.

Flirting with Danger (Book 5.5) A Sloane Monroe Short Story
A fancy hotel. A weekend getaway. For Sloane Monroe, rest has finally arrived, until the lights go out, a woman screams, and Sloane s nightmare begins.

Hush Now Baby (Book 6) (USA Today Bestselling Book)
Serena Westwood tiptoes to her baby s crib and looks inside, startled to find her newborn son is gone.

Dead of Night (Book 6.5) A Sloane Monroe Short Story
After her mother-in-law is fatally stabbed, Wren is seen fleeing with the bloody knife. Is Wren the killer, or is a dark, scandalous family secret to blame?

Gone Daddy Gone (Book 7) (USA Today Bestselling Book)
A man lurks behind Shelby in the park. Who is he? And why does he have a gun?

Smoke & Mirrors (Book 8) (USA Today Bestselling Book)
Grace Ashby wakes to the sound of a horrifying scream. She races down the hallway, finding her mother s lifeless body on the floor in a pool of blood. Her mother s boyfriend Hugh is hunched over her, but is Hugh really her mother s killer?

Sloane Monroe Stories: Deadly Sins

Deadly Sins: Sloth (Book 1)
Darryl has been shot, and a mysterious woman is sprawled out on the floor in his hallway. She s dead too. Who is she? And why have they both been murdered?

Deadly Sins: Wrath (Book 2)
Headlights flash through Maddie's car's back windshield, someone following close behind. When her car careens into a nearby tree, the chase comes to an end. But for Maddie, the end is just the beginning.

Deadly Sins: Lust (Book 3)
Marissa Calhoun sits alone on a beach-like swimming hole nestled on Australia's foreshore. Tonight, the lagoon is hers and hers alone. Or is it?

Deadly Sins: Greed (Book 4)
It was just another day for mob boss Giovanni Luciana until he took his car for a drive.

Deadly Sins: Envy (Book 5)
A cryptic message. A missing niece. And only twenty-four hours to pay.

Deadly Sins: Pride (Book 6)
A secret lies within the Kingston mansion's walls, a secret that's about to bring the past into the present.

Sloane & Maddie, Peril Awaits (Co-Authored with Janet Fix)

The Silent Boy (Book 1)
In the hallway of a local tavern, six-year-old Louie Alvarez waits for his mother to take him home. A scream rips through the air, followed by the sound of a gun being fired. Louie freezes, then turns, with a single thought on his mind: RUN.

The Shadow Children (Book 2)
Within the tunnels of the historic port city of Savannah, fourteen-year-old Andi Leland has her mind set on freedom—not just for herself but for all the other teens who have come before her.

The Broken Soul (Book 3)
When the party of a lifetime becomes a party to the death, the lines become blurred. Friends become enemies. Drugs become weapons. And that's just the beginning.

The Widow Maker (Book 4)
A friend murdered. A business in trouble. A marriage struggling to survive. And that's just the beginning.

Georgiana Germaine Series

Little Girl Lost (Book 1)
For the past two years, former detective Georgiana "Gigi" Germaine has been living off the grid, until today, when she hears some disturbing news that shakes her.

Little Lost Secrets (Book 2)
When bones are discovered inside the walls during a home renovation, Georgiana uncovers a secret that's linked to her father's untimely death thirty years earlier.

Little Broken Things (Book 3)
Twenty-year-old Olivia Spencer sits at her desk in her mother's bookshop, dreaming about her upcoming wedding. The store may be closed, but she's not alone, and her dream is about to become her worst nightmare.

Little White Lies (Book 4)
When a serial killer sweeps through the streets of Cambria, California, Georgiana Germaine gets swept up into a tangled web of deception and lies.

Little Tangled Webs (Book 5)
What if you knew the person you loved was murdered, but no one else believed you? Eighteen-year-old Harper Ellis knows she's right, and she's prepared to risk her life to prove it.

Little Shattered Dreams (Book 6)
At fifty-five, Quinn Abernathy has been through her fair share of experiences in life. And tonight, her past is coming back to haunt her.

Little Last Words (Book 7)
After living in a verbally abusive relationship for the past six years, twenty-seven-year-old Penelope Barlow has finally found the courage to leave. But can she escape ... with her life?

Little Buried Secrets (Book 8)
In a split-second, a car collides with Margot, and she finds herself hurdling through the air, her bike going one way as she goes the other. Her mind whirls in this moment, as she thinks about her life and just how much she doesn't want to die.

Little Stolen Memories (Book 9)
In a secluded cabin deep within the woods, an ominous stranger is about to change the lives of six unsuspecting teenagers forever.

Little Empty Promises (Book 10)
As librarian Cordelia Bennett prepares to lock up for the *night, a mysterious sound startles her. She turns. The fading light reveals a chilling presence in the shadows, and Cordelia realizes she's not alone.*

Addison Lockhart Series

Grayson Manor Haunting (Book 1)
When Addison Lockhart inherits Grayson Manor after her mother's untimely death, she unlocks a secret that's been kept hidden for over fifty years.

Rosecliff Manor Haunting (Book 2)
Addison Lockhart jolts awake. The dream had seemed so real. Eleven-year-old twins Vivian and Grace were so full of life, but they couldn't be. They've been dead for over forty years.

Blackthorn Manor Haunting (Book 3)
Addison Lockhart leans over the manor's window, gasping when she feels a hand on her back. She grabs the windowsill to brace herself, but it's too late--she's already falling.

Belle Manor Haunting (Book 4)
A vehicle barrels through the stop sign, slamming into the car Addison Lockhart is inside before fleeing the scene. Who is the driver of the other car? And what secrets within the walls of Belle Manor will provide the answer?

Crawley Manor Haunting (Book 5)
Something evil is coming. Something dark. Something seeking to destroy everything and everyone in its path. And Addison Lockhart is the only one who can stop it.

Till Death do us Part Novella Series

Whispers of Murder (Book 1)
It was Isabelle Donnelly's wedding day, a moment in time that should have been the happiest in her life...until it ended in murder.

Echoes of Murder (Book 2)
When two women are found dead at the same wedding, medical examiner Reagan Davenport will stop at nothing to discover the identity of the killer.

Stand-Alone Novels

Eye for Revenge (USA Today Bestselling Book)
Quinn Montgomery wakes to find herself in the hospital. Her childhood best friend Evie is dead, and Evie's four-year-old son witnessed it all. Traumatized over what he saw, he hasn't spoken.

The Perfect Lie
When true-crime writer Alexandria Weston is found murdered on the last stop of her book tour, fellow writer Joss Jax steps in to investigate.

Hickory Dickory Dead (USA Today Bestselling Book)
Maisie Fezziwig wakes to a harrowing scream outside. Curious, she walks outside to investigate, and Maisie stumbles on a grisly murder that will change her life forever.

Roadkill (USA Today Bestselling Book)
Suburban housewife Juliette Granger has been living a secret life ... a life that's about to turn deadly for everyone she loves.

Made in the USA
Middletown, DE
07 July 2024